been without imagining I have not
carnal. unimaginable.
imagining

I have been compared in appearance to Christ. the
same serenity of expression.

the fine
quality which we associate with womanhood

Christ-like
I was brought from Palestine to
a rosary. a number of knots
in a string. I would pray with that
rosary. in a chair the rosary in my hands
sunshine, trees, flowers, warmth. Outside was
nothing discordant I felt transported beyond
the mundane. heightened by prayer.

a physiological state.

a serene situation.
when I was

but not understanding. desirous

had so much trouble
When I lost courage

I could tell
I could
what I wanted this serene situation

Résumé:
Tendency to femininity
Mother dominates father.
Attached to mother. Helped her Called
sissy.

nauseating.

decidedly
. Homosexual

DENNIS C.

General impression:
On a hot afternoon Dennis comes neatly
with prominent
trousers, apparently unaware of the
mincing rotatory swaying of his hips
coy and unclear
why he has always been called Nevertheless he is delicate and
chivalrous he permits
freer play the gayest of the "queens."
Dennis has a gracile body
his embarrassment.
His capacity for grace
the small, but firm
pink cheeks
long lashes

Mississipp
I did
I had a place to sleep and eat.
I was down I used to write
I got
I was broken I tried
I couldn't keep my mind

to Sal to be the twelfth and last
these parents to start off in
poor health and poor eyesight. To these disabilities

to happen to him.

as back I let him go down

I got along
town and having affairs with men
I would get from te
othing from one affair.
s twenty
was wise to a lot then.

José has felt

José's desires

alienate José
José will emancipate

José is an attractive young man. lithe body and Lat
provocative of desire

José is also pursued by men. They "go for" him where

José is beside himself and does not know wha
(respite José)

Also by Justin Torres

We the Animals

BLACKOUTS

Farrar, Straus and Giroux
New York

BLACKOUTS

A Novel

JUSTIN TORRES

Farrar, Straus and Giroux
120 Broadway, New York 10271

Excerpts from this novel previously appeared in different form as
"Reverting to a Wild State" and "Leashed" in *The New Yorker*; "Starve a Rat" in
Harper's Magazine; and "It Had to Be Gold," first in *Los Angeles Times' Image*
magazine and later in *The Best American Essays 2022*.

Grateful acknowledgment is made for permission to reprint the following material:
Excerpt from "Now and then" from *Collected Poems*, by James Schuyler.
Copyright © 1993 by the Estate of James Schuyler. Reprinted by permission of
Farrar, Straus and Giroux. All rights reserved.
Excerpt from "The Cage of Voices" from *Collected Poems* (Holt, Rinehart & Winston),
by Horace Gregory. Copyright © 1964 by the Estate of Horace Gregory.
Used with permission.

Illustration credits can be found on pages 303–305.

Library of Congress Cataloging-in-Publication Data
Names: Torres, Justin, 1980– author.
Title: Blackouts : a novel / Justin Torres.
Description: First edition. | New York : Farrar, Straus and Giroux, 2023.
Identifiers: LCCN 2023015272 | ISBN 9780374293574 (hardcover)
Subjects: LCGFT: Novels.
Classification: LCC PS3620.O5897 B55 2023 | DDC 813/.6—
    dc23/eng/20230407
LC record available at https://lccn.loc.gov/2023015272

Designed by Gretchen Achilles

Our books may be purchased in bulk for promotional, educational,
or business use. Please contact your local bookseller or the Macmillan Corporate
and Premium Sales Department at 1-800-221-7945, extension 5442, or by email at
MacmillanSpecialMarkets@macmillan.com.

www.fsgbooks.com
www.twitter.com/fsgbooks • www.facebook.com/fsgbooks

1   3   5   7   9   10   8   6   4   2

I dedicate this book to
VALENCIA MARTINEZ *& to*
MY DAVID,
THE MOST BRILLIANT AND MOST USEFUL
I HAVE EVER MET

BLACKOUTS

[REDACTED] Poetry
loses some of its charm through the suggestion that it might be an
expression of the writer's sexual maladjustment. But as a matter of
fact it is beginning to seem that all imaginative writings are attempts
to find libidinous satisfaction in fantasy. [REDACTED]

[REDACTED] The author has [REDACTED]
[REDACTED] tendencies; [REDACTED] has
made no attempt to estimate what proportion of imaginative writing
may be the work of [REDACTED] confined [REDACTED] self; [REDACTED]
[REDACTED] has accepted the fact that human beings reveal themselves
in whatever they read and write. [REDACTED]

GEORGE W. HENRY, M.D.

I

THE PALACE

There was a time
when I didn't know
anyone who was dead—
let alone any ghosts.
—**JAIME MANRIQUE**, "Ghosts and the Living"

I came to the Palace because the man I sought kept a room there. He stood at the point of egress, supporting himself against the door frame, not just thin, but skeletal; lips shrunken and chapped; the skin of his face pulled taut over the skull. I led him back to the bed, where he looked at me, kind yet wild. His eyes burned with life, as if the spirit had left the flesh and concentrated there, in irises bright and glassy, the milk of the whites unsullied. His voice, though fey, came hale and lucid, and when he spoke, he did so without obstruction, no wheezing, no confusion (that is, until the final hours, when he slipped into delirium, speaking nonsense and quoting from literature). I told him I would stay, play bed nurse, however long it took. The truth is I had nowhere else to go, and both of us knew as much. Juan insisted that, after his death, I remain in the Palace and take over his room. He asked that I finish the project that had once consumed him, the story of a certain woman who shared his last name. Miss Jan Gay. "Come," he said with a wink, "squeeze mother's hands as a sign you will do it." This was an allusion to some famous scene I could not place; it was not a joke. I took his hands, all knuckles and finger bones, into my own. He was near death, and I would have promised him anything.

"*I had never meant to keep my promise. But before I knew it my head began to swim with dreams* . . . What's that from?"

"I don't know, Juan. But I will keep this one. I mean to."

"Some call her one thing, some another," he said. "Yahn, or Jan, or Helen. Holy fairy, mother of grace. Our Father who art in between."

However, many homosexuals fail to survive the rigors of warfare the constant intimate association with men.

I had ventured off to the Palace with the last of my money, alone after all had been lost to the metropolis. I had no work, no degree and no pedigree, no feel for the game, no man to support me. I bought a ticket for a bus headed west, to a small city thousands of miles and several days away—to the place where I suspected Juan might have retreated. I carried a single duffel bag stuffed with clothes. Hour upon hour, I watched the landscape change, through windows filmed over with grease. When once I tried to rub clean the view, using the edge of my sleeve, I instead created a halation effect, like the Vaseline smudge of an Old Hollywood close-up. There I was, nose unscarred, black curls tamed, every hard feature softened in reflection.

Along the way, we cycled through buses and drivers, one of whom was an appealing man, brown and burly. His smiling eyes twinkled in the rearview mirror, and he announced each stop with folksy joviality. As seats came available, I found myself moving forward from the back, nearer and nearer, until I was directly to his right, only slightly behind, close enough to notice the hairs sprouting on either side of his knuckles. *Watch*, he said to me, *this whole bus is about to empty. Our last stop before we cross the Big Muddy.* And so it came to pass, everyone piled out; he and I alone made the crossing. The river was wide and rushing and indeed muddy, a milky chocolate color, which reminded me of Easter holidays, of bunnies wrapped in foil with lifeless, sugar-candy eyes. He asked where I was headed, and I told him, and he said, *Well, it won't be me who takes you there.* And then his mood changed and he dropped the act, simply nodding at those who boarded. When the new driver arrived—pallid, officious—I felt not exactly frightened, but less brave. Chilled. *Journeys end in lovers meeting* played in my mind, but where I'd picked up the dreadful line, some book, or film, or nursery rhyme, I could not recall. I returned to a seat in the back. The people who boarded at the stops thereafter were of a different sort—they seemed to me exotic, interior, anti-coastal—and then the landscape really began to flatten and the visible horizon expanded in every direction, so that the sky grew bigger and more vaulted, and I found I could look and look forever into the desert, and never tire of the new earthy pigments—new, at least, to me— the pinks and coppers and sand and clay.

We arrived in the early morning, and I disembarked, hoping to hitch a ride from there, but very few cars passed. For several hours, I stood on the side of the road beside a small mesquite tree. The paltry shade dissipated with the noontime sun, and the dust caught in my throat. When what I counted to be the fiftieth car whipped by, I began to despair, but then came a vision of brake lights and the crunch of tires pulling onto the gravel shoulder. European tourists, a couple. *You do not cut a particularly threatening figure*, the man said. He offered to take me all the way. The woman scowled; I realized they had been fighting and that I was to serve as a diversion, so I chattered a bit, though it wasn't long before she picked up the thread of their argument in a hushed and accusatory foreign language and I returned to the landscape.

And so we pushed on, farther into the desert, to an even smaller city, a village really, in search of the Palace, in search of Juan, until I found him, a skeleton in the entranceway.

In another life, Juan and I had only known each other for a total of eighteen days, nearly a decade before, when I was just seventeen. Even then, he felt frail, though sharp of mind, and so attentive. At that time, my own grandparents were still relatively young, in their late fifties, and so I had no experience with the elderly, as I considered Juan to be, and I was made nervous by the dry and mottled skin of Juan's arms and hands, the manifold creases at the corners of his lips and eyes. "My senescence," Juan called it. "An affront to youth and beauty." And though I knew he teased, I did feel repulsed, not by Juan himself, but by elderliness as abstraction. I found it impossible to imagine my own adolescent body succumbing to old age, deteriorating. Back then, I had looked at Juan and thought, *No way that body is my future.*

The Palace rose monumental from the dusty street. A desert building fallen into disrepair. The once-white stucco a dirty ivory color, here and there chipped away, exposing the brick beneath. I don't know how the nickname came to be; there are no palaces in this country. It would have been a hotel, or a stately asylum, once upon a time. The roof's wide eaves were supported by carved corbels, and above the entrance, at the peak of the facade, a cutout had been sculpted in the shape of a three-leaf clover, which reminded me of the ace of clubs from a deck of playing cards, and which may have been a bell gable once, though no bell hung inside now, only framed azure sky. The marble staircases had worn yellow, the interior spaces haphazardly subdivided into smaller rooms with painted plaster walls and mismatched trim. Grand doors were bolted shut and whitewashed. I had no idea who ran the Palace; a charity, I assumed, a place for those without family. Juan had his own room, a desk, a miniature refrigerator, a hot plate, a small closet, and a twin bed low to the floor. Books ran along the baseboards. Juan was allowed visitors for certain hours in the morning and afternoon, but kept his window cracked, and at night I shimmied up the fire escape and snuck back inside and sat on the edge of his mattress. We talked. I had many questions, and many hours with nowhere to be. Some nights I spent with men, tricks I picked up in the village bar, the Depot, next to the bus station. Or else I picked them up by lurking around the bus lot itself, or cruising the toilets, but soon I found I wanted only to be in the room, with Juan. I liked best to spend the night in the bed beside him, where I could feel his bones and papery skin, and breathe in his rotten breath, and know he hadn't left.

Juan did not think much of the other residents, wandering souls, whom he referred to as a *badling* of queer ducks. I'd never before heard that collective noun. "All bitter," he said, "or broken. Or lunatic." The kitchen, the communal toilets, the showers—nowhere in the building ventilated properly; instead the rooms held the residents' scents, musk and shit and grime and scorched food. Juan preferred not to venture beyond his own door. He ate only canned soup, tomato and cream, or lentil, which I heated for him, setting the can directly on the hot plate. I'd prop him up and watch as he spooned from can to mouth with tremulous deliberation. Afterward, while we talked, he picked at the wallpaper by the side of the bed as carefully as his fingers allowed. "Just underneath, the paper is all the more beautiful," he said. He'd uncovered a patch the size of a dinner plate, the pattern a circus scene drawn in a delicate, old-fashioned style: pink poodles leaping through a hoop; an elephant balanced on one leg atop a small stool; hobos clowning each other. "I'd like to excavate the entire wall before I die, but I won't, will I?"

I did not talk about after; instead I told little lies about the future. "One of these days, I am going to get you a pot. And a bowl. And watch you eat with dignity."

The grand project, which I was to complete after Juan's death, involved a file folder stuffed with scraps of paper, newspaper clippings, photographs, and scribbled notes, along with two massive books whose pages had been mostly blacked out. The books comprised a research study, published in two volumes and titled *Sex Variants: A Study of Homosexual Patterns*.

Right away, I felt the magnetism, the mystery of these books; a work of intense observation transformed into a work of erasure. And I wondered about Juan's connection to Miss Jan Gay, mentioned in the introduction. I asked Juan if he and she were blood. "No, no." And yet, he told me, I was right to believe their connection "ran deeper than nominal similarity." That was all he said.

I couldn't understand why, but once I arrived, and once the promise to continue the work had been extracted, Juan seemed to lose interest in the books himself; he turned his face to the wall, to the wallpaper, and I found it difficult to get him to explain anything. Still, I prodded with questions about the research study, about the sex variants described therein, about Jan Gay, about who had blacked out all the pages, and why, and was it Juan himself? "No, no." He'd found the books that way, erased into little poems and observations. He insinuated he would tell me more, in time, but first, he wanted to know about me and my life in the decade since we'd last seen each other. Juan knew just how to get me to talk, despite myself; the words pulled forth as if through hypnotic force.

Juan worried over me. The Palace, he claimed, attracted those undone by trouble. He suggested, with sincerity, that I was on the lam, but this was another figure of speech with which I was unfamiliar, and even after he explained, the entire notion of running and hiding seemed funny to me, as old-fashioned as the wallpaper.

"Running from who? The cops? Bookies? A pimp?"

"From whom," Juan said. And after a moment he added, "Your mind, then."

The hemp of the bedside lampshade warmed the light so that his brown eyes burned a rapturous color, liquor-like. I couldn't get over how they shone, the incongruence, the rest of his face a death mask.

Downtown, around the Palace, the buildings and the roads held the day's heat and radiated warmth through the night. Infernal nights with no escape. The bed was small. The ceiling fan worked only at the slowest speed.

"As if everything here is permanently set to some languorous tempo, eh, nene?" Juan said. "The fan and the air, you and I, time itself."

I strutted about the room naked down to my white cotton underwear. I only ever dressed to go outside, and even then I didn't wear much. Beyond keeping cool, I hoped to give Juan a thrill, but he rarely flirted. He kept himself covered in the thin bedsheet, though I'd seen his body many times, helping him out of bed and down the hall to the toilet. At first, I turned away from the shock of his skeleton, but over time I grew accustomed to his emaciation, and I would watch as the bones and joints moved under the skin with uncanny and fearsome beauty.

Juan himself gave off very little body heat, but on the hottest nights any skin contact at all, no matter how slight, proved insufferable, and I would move from the bed to the hard floor. Sleep was impossible; we didn't try. Instead, Juan's voice floated down to me. He liked to guide me into a trance, and he was good at it; so good, I felt that one of those nights I might not recover.

Tell me, again, about the blackout that led to the flood. Close your eyes. What do you see?"

"I'm back home, in the city. Just about finished cleaning up. The dishes all washed and left to dry, except for a heavy stockpot that needs soaking. I'd cooked this large, nostalgic meal—all for myself—and then found I had no appetite, so I packed it all away. I place the pot in the sink, turn on the tap. I think, *Let the basin fill.*"

"Then nothing?"

"Nothingness."

In the front room, I look down to where the water trickles in. A snaking rivulet hits the sofa leg, parts, rejoins. Somewhere, my landlady screams murder. *He's done it*, I think. Screams rise up from below, from the place where she lives. I startle awake, though technically awake already, standing upright; I startle back into the self. Run to the kitchen, water pours down from the counter, water spreads across the floor, two inches deep, and then comes a groaning, ungodly. The landlords' bedroom sits directly below, and it's their ceiling groaning, buckling in, ripping open. I don't see, but hear: the plaster, the ceiling fan, and the light fixture all come crashing down.

Up the stairs, the landlady pounds on my door, screaming my name, crying out to Jesucristo, screaming about the water and what have I done? Open the door—the way she looks at me then, looks through me—tell her: *It's done, it's over.* She scrambles around throwing down towels, sheets, the duvet, anything to absorb the water; I'm apologizing, a mistake, I left the tap running. She doesn't seem to hear. The next thing I remember is following her downstairs, to her bedroom, and there's the husband. Cool as a crocodile, eating. He sits on the only little corner of the bed still dry, eating—something off the bone. Not chicken; oxtail, maybe, or lamb. They would have been in the middle of dinner. The bed is covered in muck, and it's just awful, the damage. Wet tongues of ceiling plaster hang down. The hole above. Straight through to the beams that separate us, to the undersides of my floorboards. In the cracks, I can see the light from my kitchen; the water continues to drip, gently now, down onto the mattress, the dresser. The husband's cool seems a rebuke of the wife, who wails, real, big, wet tears. I can't really understand everything she says, a lot of it idiomatic, but I get the gist—she wants an explanation, not from me, but from God it seems, how could I do such a thing? The guilt I feel is so acute it makes me light-headed, but impossible to look away from the husband, the eating. Repulsive. His silence, I realize, is directed at me, as if searching for just the right hex, the right way to condemn me to hell. I'm afraid I will be sick. Though it's as if he can't see me either, or at least, he won't look at me. He looks dead forward, and he chews.

What is it? Why do you stop?"

"The dish I left to soak in the sink. Not a stockpot . . . I can't remember the correct word."

"That's because you hardly speak a lick of Spanish, nene. You never bothered to learn, did you?"

"Well, I mean, my father . . ."

"Your father what?"

"He spoke the language, but at us, not with us. You know?"

"I see. Blame the old man. The old man blames you. No one has to teach, or learn."

"Tell me the word."

"El caldero. Like a witch. Now go on. Close your eyes."

"I guess the next thing I see is the cleanup. Hours and hours. Hauling the wet plaster out to the curb. Heavy-duty black plastic bags filled with sopping filth. The house is very old, the plaster-work original. In the mess, a clump of photographs, which must have been on the bureau, or the floor by the bed, and which the landlady now takes and gingerly peels one from another, setting to dry atop a tea towel stretched across the radiator. Many, clearly, are ruined. Old pictures, from her island days, black-and-white prints on photo paper with white borders and scalloped edges. Irreplaceable. Every time she looks up to ceiling, to the floor above, my floor, I wince. I wish I could describe the look on her face."

"Try."

"Oh, I don't know . . . how do you describe an expression? The tension in her face and neck released, her cheeks and eyebrows and lips all slid down, her chin dipped . . . I don't know what the word is . . . crestfallen, I suppose."

"A fine word."

"Where does it come from? I'm sure you know."

"Well, cocks have crests, and other birds, and horses."

"And mountains."

"And mountains. And waves. And the houses of great families."

"And they all fall down?"

"That's right, the mountains crumble, and the waves crash, and they all fall down—the chickens and the horses and the families and the faces of the landladies. But go on, keep describing the blackout."

"When will it be your turn? I came here to find you."

"I came to Comala because I had been told that my father lived there . . ."

"Comala. What is that? I know that. I knew that, once."

"Soon it will be my turn, but first you must give me the whole story. It's very important to get the details right."

"About the landlady?"

"About the blackout, the flood, everything that brought you here."

José has felt

José's desires

alienate José José will emancipate himself

José is an attractive young man. lithe body and Latin blood provocative of desire

José is also pursued by men. They "go for" him wherever he goes.

José is beside himself and does not know what he will do. (respite José)

José is harassed by homosexuals. The world is going crazy." José might as well do as he wishes.

The landlady's screams had not reached me directly. Several moments passed until I startled out of my reverie, though on the edges, I felt the screaming; it echoed somewhere deep in my mind. When inside the blackout, I remembered, or relived, and sometimes I relived lives that were not my own. I was somewhere else, with someone else. A woman, a scream, and a great silencing.

"Do you understand?"

"Help me to. Go on."

"The water must have pooled for an hour, at least; the material damage ran to thousands of dollars, all that water, me just standing there, in the front room with the faucet running and my mind . . . where? Because I don't understand. I remember I heard the voice, the screams, curdling screams, but at the same time I stood very still, as if I were listening to something, or for someone, some violence, beyond the screams. I'm not talking about the husband. Oh no. Both of them so old, and sure, maybe he's silent and sulky, compared to her—a wonderful woman, very kind and chatty, a teetotaler, very religious, but not in the punitive, fire-and-brimstone sense of that word, which was familiar enough to me, but in a charitable, spiritual sense I'd never before experienced—anyway, no, I don't think he had such passions. I don't think he beat her. Maybe once, but not anymore. Some other violence I was listening out for. I remember, just before coming around, that I felt, or I had the thought, *Now he's gone and offed himself.*"

"And who is he?"

"That's what I'm asking."

"And now, do you know where you are?"

"I'm here with you. And you've got this project. All this ephemera stuffed into a manila folder, and the books, and that little bundle of photographs tied with string. And you're going to show and tell, fill in the gaps. Isn't that right?"

"And if the gaps are too many to be filled? What then?"

"Do you know how long I've been here, Juan? Already?"

"Tomorrow will be my turn to speak."

"So you keep saying."

"Tomorrow and tomorrow and tomorrow. The way to dusty death."

It was in an institution that Juan and I had met. At the time I was still several months shy of my eighteenth birthday, but I'd been deemed too mature for juvey, and so they fudged the rules and housed me with the adults. Back then, I felt somehow proud to be insane in an adult way, though now, in the stifling room, that world felt further away in both space and time, and I saw how young and immature I must have seemed to Juan. *The past is a foreign country*, Juan would say, quoting, and indeed back there, in that other place, they do things differently. Juan and I had been wards of the state, kept under constant observation.

From the moment I arrived, I was met with rules, a litany of regulatory proclamations. I shivered on a chair before the intake nurse, trying to grasp my change in circumstance. I kept quiet, meek, tracing the pattern of pinprick ventilation in the dingy suede of my sneakers, unable to make eye contact, to utter even a word of protest. The entire scene felt like a copy of a copy of a bad script, one I recognized from television and books. Everything, from the nurse's icy demeanor to my own timidity and dread—all of it a cliché little drama that must have played out in that very room countless times. I tried to observe the scene as if outside myself, focusing on the details, the ventilated suede, the scratch of the pen, the boredom in the nurse's voice.

Only when the nurse deployed the phrase *privy privacy*, without any sense of irony, did I find there was still enough of the teenager in me to snicker.

Oh yes, nene, I remember the entire spiel. During the initial seventy-two hours, the ward may not go to the bathroom, or shower, alone . . ."

". . . After that, privileges are earned . . ."

". . . This is good behavior, this is bad behavior . . ."

". . . This is the doorknob, no lock . . ."

". . . Barricading the door with a chair, like this, is bad behavior . . ."

". . . This is the shower timer; please be outside the curtain before the buzzer . . ."

". . . Safety razors, toenail clippers, sharps of any kind will be kept under lock and key and only allowed with supervised use . . ."

". . . The same with personal, corded things, like headphones and shoelaces . . ."

". . . Please remove both shoelaces now . . . Please. And now . . .

". . . Otherwise, I will have to go down onto the hard floor with my knees, stiff as they are . . ."

". . . Noncompliance is bad behavior . . ."

". . . You've only just been admitted, do you really want to begin with a black mark?"

After the unpleasantness with the laces, which I neither resisted nor abetted, came a kind of inquisition. The personal history. An inventory of bad thoughts and deeds. The nurse was softly butch, perhaps in her fifties, but I was too shy, or stubborn, to look directly at her. Instead, I stared into the middle space. The psychiatric unit sat deep in the building's interior; a male orderly had wheeled me there, in a chair, up one elevator, down the hall, up another. I never turned to look, never saw any more of the man than his two square hands. He smelled familiar—thick with smoke and tar—the way one smells just after a cigarette break. The orderly had hummed the whole way, "Put on a Happy Face," at times breaking into a soft whistle, and the tune did not feel like a taunt, but a kindness.

Along the way, I kept an eye out for a window, or a door to the outside, but we passed none. This room, intake, was windowless as well. The only furnishings were the nurse's mobile cart and two chairs, which had cracked everywhere, like hardened rubber, yet held sturdy. The room had been set up to tolerate human filth, to be easily cleansed, though dark streaks and pockmarks marred the walls—evidence of struggle, meltdowns, resistance. A file folder lay open on the nurse's lap; question after question. The nurse granted no special care to her appearance, her hair loosely pulled back, her uniform somewhat oversized, misshapen, and yet she seemed especially clean, next to me. I felt a twinge of shame for having sent her down onto her knees, but I pushed the thought away, then pushed away the next image: my folks. *This is hard*, my mother had said, but not to me, to a doctor. Finally, the questions were over, and I was taken to a bed. The nurse sat sentinel in the room through the night, with the light on. Unlike on television, the walls were not padded.

Sometime very deep into the night, the nurse came and told me, "You can't go on shaking like that." I was unaware I'd been shivering. She said, "I can give you something." *What?* I wanted to ask. *What can you give to me?* Only I turned my face to the wall, allowed her to pinch the fat of my arm, then nothing. Nothingness.

Do you sleep now, nene? Are you back there?"

"No, not yet, Juan. But yes."

On the second night, the nurse was there at my bedside, with the light on. Sleep was, again, impossible; I asked to be allowed to sit at the table in the common room and draw. Technically this was forbidden, but she nodded in a neutral sort of way, helped me out of bed—I was surprised to be a bit wobbly on my feet. The medicines, I supposed. The nurse settled me at the round table. She was the same one, the soft butch, but much younger than I'd thought, maybe only in her thirties, with the local habit of raising and lengthening the short *a* sound, almost making two syllables out the word *trap*, which is to say, white working class, and I wondered if, somewhere underneath, she was kind, or kin, or one with whom I ought to be wary. I asked for pen and paper, and she sourced both, then pulled a chair away from the table and sat directly behind, out of my line of sight, but between me and the only exit. Perhaps she read a magazine. Certainly not a book. I noticed there were no books in that place, or at least no literature, only thick medical texts on the shelves behind the nurses' stand, layered in dust.

I drew, and the drawing turned out to be a fairly heavy-handed allegory: an ornately carved chair with plush seats and clawed feet; with straps for restraining the arms and legs, and one of those metal skullcaps hooked up to a tangle of cables, except in the shape of a crown. A throne, wired for electrocution.

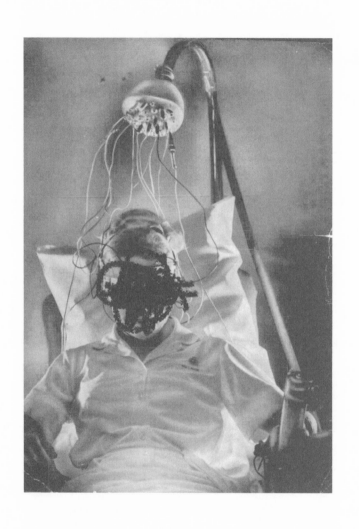

I didn't know quite why, but over the course of a year or so, I'd become obsessed with chairs. Several months before, in high school art class, I'd fabricated a chair out of plywood—almost, but not quite, large enough for an adult to sit. I'd hand-painted the thing a green umbra, using acrylic and epoxy, so that it looked mildewed, wet. Screws drilled in from the back—all down the spine—poked through to the front, like spikes, and a single over-sized screw came up from the seat. The effect was not so much a chair, I realized, but a perversion.

After that, the art teacher, a sculptor himself, had taken an interest in me, privately taught me to weld, at a station set up behind the loading dock, purportedly for the teacher's personal use. The school did not have liability insurance enough to cover students wielding torches; the lessons were a secret between us. He was from a Southern state—one of the few people in that town, outside my parents, who didn't speak in the flat regional accent, and the only teacher of color I'd ever had in all my years of schooling. The first and best thing I'd welded was a very tall, very narrow chair, perhaps eight inches wide and four feet high. In the Arts section of the newspaper, I'd happened across an image of a gray old man and a gray old woman, in a gray room with a gray table and gray chairs, and all around them were plaster cats painted radioactive green. I didn't understand whether the man and woman were alive or sculptures. At seventeen, I'd never seen anything like it. So I sculpted a little mummified human out of newspaper and wire, wrapped in plaster of Paris, to sit on the welded throne. The plaster was bright white, and the human fig-ure obscenely narrow and long; it sat gripping the armrests, with its head tilted to the side, and one leg crossed over the other. A provocative pose. A few years before, the world had gone crazy over a famous actress crossing and uncrossing her legs, and ever so briefly flashing her naked crotch in a room full of men, all of them interrogators. She wore a very short white dress. I stole some essence from that scene, from her pose, without realizing, until the art teacher pointed to the similarity. I had titled the sculpture *The Shrink*.

The old couple and the cats in the gray room. Do you remember?"

"I'm afraid I don't, no."

"Well, I remember meeting you very clearly. And everything
we said."

"Don't rush ahead."

"Okay, Juan. Let's see . . . I spend that first week in a kind
of catatonic silence, refusing to participate in group, to speak to
the doctors, to speak to any human really. Only at night, when
absolutely alone, do I sometimes try to converse with the night
nurse. She never yields to much conversation. There are no more
injections, only sleeping pills, which take an hour or so to kick
in, and in that time, the nurse indulges my drawing. She's even
found for me a sketchbook, left behind by another patient, she
claims, though it's never been used, no pages filled or missing, and
I choose to believe she bought the sketchbook for me herself, with
her own money. No idea what makes me think that—narcissism,
I suppose, or my desperation to be looked after—"

"But who can tell the difference."

"But who can tell the difference. Each morning my mind is so
thick, I can barely chew breakfast—the pills, I think—but anyway
the food disgusts me. They keep track of what is left on my tray,
and if I don't eat enough, I'm forced to drink a lukewarm can
of Ensure. That first day, between meals and group therapy, you
come and sit on the bench and say nothing alongside me."

"I must have seemed very strange to you then."

"Ancient. Breakable."

"Charming."

"Anyway, after several days of sitting together in silence, I finally speak. I describe the picture I once saw in the newspaper: this old gray couple in a room full of cats. I describe it in great detail, how the woman wears a smock, how both are hunched with age. I add that here, in the nuthouse, I somehow feel myself to be living inside that photo. As if you and I are the old couple, and all the nutjobs are the cats, crawling and sniffing about us. You really don't remember?"

"Not at all. And what do I say?"

"Nothing. Only you smile, and let out a gentle laugh, just air pushed quickly through the nostrils. I could have kissed you."

"And why do you think I came to sit with you?"

"I assumed it was because of the resemblance."

"Tribalism?"

"I guess. I mean, we both have a bit too much forehead, don't we? And whiskey-colored eyes—that's what Liam used to say, my ex, about my eyes. But I don't just mean ethnicity, or skin tone; the resemblance is deeper, it carries over to manner as well, doesn't it?"

"Yes, I suppose it does. How shall we describe that manner? A too-lightness, an air of vacancy?"

"You told me you were just about my age the first time you were committed."

"Oh, I shouldn't have said that."

"You told me you'd had all kinds of treatments, that you'd developed a dependence on electroshock in particular. By the age of forty, you said, you'd been relieved of libido altogether."

"And did you understand?"

"Not then, no. The words I understood, sure, but not how you meant them."

"The release of the want of the want of release. Though, as it turns out, libido was the last defense I had."

"I'm still not sure I understand. Defense against what?"

"Well, your nothingness, I suppose."

"Have you had many lovers, Juan? I wouldn't be surprised."

"Never mind. Go on with the story."

"I remember studying you. I remember the veins visible across the backs of your hands, and your fingers, long and thin, the tips stained yellow from tobacco. I felt none of the unease of masculinity in you. I knew that you had loved this woman, an artist, your adoptive mother, and that she haunted you still. At first, I thought she'd abandoned you, but I came to realize that was imprecise; actually, I got the sense that the adoption had failed, and the failure had broken your heart, but that the woman herself remained blameless in your eyes. If anything, you took responsibility for failing her . . . Won't you tell me anything? About the woman? Zhenya?"

"I can tell you I did not know her very long. Though you and I didn't know each other very long, either, did we? And yet here you are, haunting me."

"Eighteen days."

"Close your eyes. Go back there, be in that place, on that bench. Tell me, what do you feel?"

"Lost. But also watched. And watched over."

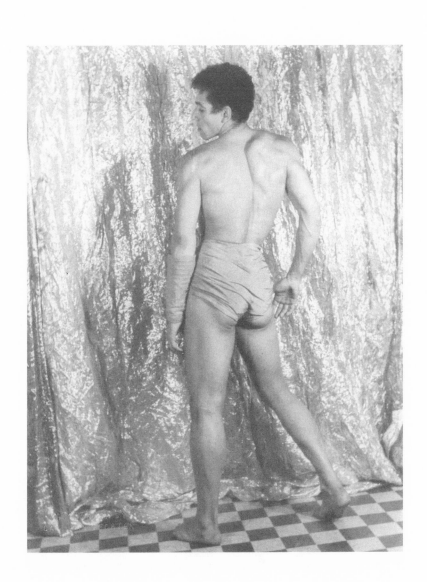

At first, I'd known him by a false name. The nurses all called him John. Only days later, after we broke our silence, did I notice his medical bracelet read JUAN GAY, a name I found discordant, but also amusing.

When I asked why the nurses did not use his real name, Juan explained that he'd been in and out of that place for decades. A few of the staff knew him from way back, a time when every even slightly foreign name was Americanized. The false name had carried over from the older nurses to newer ones. Juan never much cared what they thought, or what they called him; he never felt a need to correct the misapprehensions of others. Even then I had thought he seemed free, though of course neither of us were allowed to venture any farther than the locked double doors at the end of the hall.

Juan was deeply reserved and much older than the other patients, and I was deeply terrified and much younger. We sat side by side in a quiet corner on a pine bench, thickly glossed, with turned and painted legs. At first, we did not speak very much. In our silent communion, we faced down the immense stretches of gray boredom. On occasion, the rebellious adolescent spirit might flare up, and I would want to lash out, cause a scene, but I wanted more Juan's presence beside me, so I stayed quiet and still and used the edge of my thumbnail to carve a curse into the bench, pressing so hard my wrist throbbed in the night.

Such a gentle old man. Later, I would learn all manner of vocabulary to think about sex, and gender, but invoking any of those words would be anachronistic—I was a teenager from bumfuck nowhere; I saw only that Juan transcended what I thought I knew about sissies. When he spoke, he spoke in allusion, literarily, often pausing to check, with a look, whether I followed. I don't think he expected me to understand directly, but rather wanted me to understand how little I knew about myself, that I was missing out on something grand: a subversive, variant culture; an inheritance.

Side by side. Me slightly feverish with rage, and with shame, and with questions unasked. Juan waited me out, watched over me, and at the same time, I felt he was somewhere else, as if we both were witnesses to other happenings; loops from the past playing and replaying in our minds. Not only did Juan have a rather severe tremor, but a twitch as well, which jerked his head to the side at regular intervals. His eyes perpetually teared. "Honestly," he said one morning, "it's the medications, and the treatments, and age . . . this failing body." Then he crossed his arms, and pushed out his bottom lip, mocking a toddler's pout. "I ain't cry. Not never over nothing."

"Do you know, back in that place, one evening you told me all about Rimbaud? I assumed from your pronunciation that the name was spelled like the movie, *Rambo*. Afterward, I couldn't find any books in the library."

"Oh, don't let's be maudlin."

"I am. I mean . . . sentimental, at least, about the way you were. Not just what you would say, but how you listened. So closely. At times you closed your eyes tight and held them like that for several moments longer than felt comfortable. I liked you very much. I wanted to steal your style. You had this kind of sloppiness about you."

"I prefer the term *corporeal disregard.*"

[41]

"Well, I wanted to steal that . . . disregard. And I wanted to steal, too, your cultured, gentle regard for others."

"A young hoodlum who let himself be taken by the pimps—in order to steal their ego. That's Sartre, describing Jean Genet."

"That's right. That's exactly right, I wanted to steal your ego. God, I was miserable then. Mortified by my own body. I wanted to leap up out of my skin. I wanted to know things."

I worked as a longshoreman on a Mississippi line ████ I returned to Miami. ██████████████ I did ██████████ I didn't like it. ████████████ I had a place to sleep and eat. ████████ I was down ███ I used to write ████████████████████████████████████ I got a telegram ████████ I was broken ████████████████ I tried to work ████ █████████ I couldn't keep my mind ████████ ██ I quit ███ I was fired █████████████████████

I couldn't think about sex. I didn't have enough to eat to think about it. ████████████████████████████████ ██████ I wanted to make a couple of dollars in the men's room. ███ ██████████████████████████████ I didn't like the idea. ███████ I went West and rambled all over ███████ ████████ I met a Jewish fellow ███████████████████ ████████████ I went to New York ████ I met this Jewish fellow again. ████████████████████████████ █████████████████████████████ I did. I hit him lightly ██████████████████████ I hit him hard enough to make it red. ████████████ I thought he was a detective ███████████████ I got a room for a week. ████████ █ I had some underwear. ████████████ ██ I didn't. ████ I lay on my back and he put it in between my legs. ███████████████ I would let him brown me. I met someone else ████████████████████████████ ████████ I was back █████████ I let him go down on me. ██████ I started going ████████████████████ I was crazy ██████████████████ I got along all right. I kept batting around town and having affairs with men █████████ ████████████████████. I would get from ten to twenty dollars and some clothing from one affair. ████████ ██████ I was twenty ████████████████ I was wise to a lot then. ████████████

In the stale air of the hot room of the Palace, in the presence of death, my own body radiated a kind of shameless vitality; I grew vain and easily aroused. Twenty-seven. Afire. Proud about my "lithe body and Latin blood," about looking much younger than my age, though still morbidly embarrassed by my smile, which showed too much of my gums—like a dog, a trick once said—and my broken and browning front teeth. Terribly uncultured as well. While Juan slept, which was most hours of the day, I peacocked about the room, shades drawn, no reflection in the glass; I imagined myself irresistible, alive.

"I once had a shot at refinement, you know."

"Is that so?"

"Yes. A scholarship to a fine, expensive university."

"And what happened there?"

"Things with me were chaotic. I'd just gotten out of the asylum. I was too much distracted to stay. I lasted one month."

"And perhaps, nene, you romanticized it all?"

"What all?"

"Well, the failure. The sharp slick thing you were allowing yourself to become. The very idea of the hoodlum homosexual."

On the eighteenth day, a distracted nurse left three full prescription bottles out on the counter, which I swiped. Antidepressants, antipsychotics, sedatives, ninety pills in total. I spent an hour choking them down, one or two at a time, still childishly poor at swallowing medicine. I was found, as I must have known I would be found, in the nick of time, and whisked away to intensive care, where I spent several days comatose. A machine beat my heart and pumped air into and out of my lungs. When I came out of the coma and for the next two weeks I had no short-term memory. I'd ask the same questions on a loop, where was I and why and what was the date and how much time had I lost? My memory returned, but damaged. After I was well enough to transfer, they sent me to yet another place entirely, much dingier than the last. Months later, I finally checked out of the last hospital, and soon after, a package arrived. Inside, I found a clear plastic bag with my shoelaces, clothes, and other personal effects, along with a small gold crucifix on a golden chain, which had not belonged to me.

I tried to remember, had I noticed the occasional flash of a chain peeking above the collar of Juan's undershirt? I couldn't be sure. I'd mostly stared down to the floor, or at his hands, and I wished then that I had looked closer at Juan, memorized his kingly face before it vanished.

The last image from that place:

We two rise from the bench, summoned to lunch. Our final day together, though neither can know. Juan places a hand on my shoulder for balance. We'd spent the morning entirely in silence, but then, out of nowhere, Juan speaks, not as if opening a conversation, but closing one. He is always quoting literature and films, and when he speaks to me in Spanish, he speaks slowly and crisply so I might catch the words and, with time, their meaning.

"Yo creo que los reyes desaparecen," he says.

For ten years, nene, you forgot me entirely."

"And then, Juan, you came rushing back."

"All at once?"

"Like a flood."

"Après moi, le déluge."

In Juan's room, in the Palace, the ancient cast-iron radiator was fitted over the top with a metal covering, making a small shelf where, at some point when he was more mobile, Juan had placed the two volumes of *Sex Variants: A Study of Homosexual Patterns*. No other books stood on the shelf, only those two upright volumes, identical in form, cloth hardbacks with embossed gold titling, whose thick black parallel spines reminded me of twin towers. Inside, the pages were yellowed and ready to crumble. The first volume was called simply *MEN*, and the second *WOMEN*, though the stories within complicated the ease of that binary.

MEN and *WOMEN* were further subdivided into three categories: *Bisexual Cases*, *Homosexual Cases*, and *Narcissistic Cases*.

How to describe the shock of opening the first book, *MEN*? I opened the book carelessly, not realizing the glue along the spine had deteriorated, and the pages spilled out helter-skelter across the floor, many of them nearly covered in black marker. At first glance, the blackouts seemed like the scribblings of a demented mind, and then I thought maybe they were redactions made by some state functionary, until I noticed the precision and painstaking effort, the obsessive care, went beyond mere censorship. All that vanished text. Not a pleasant surprise, but a deep surprise, an intrigue. I told Juan the erasures were a provocation, but the word echoed, a false note.

Comment:

to Sal to be the twelfth and last child of these parents to start off in life with poor health and poor eyesight. To these disabilities

to happen to him.

to the age of seven when he became aware of a desire to press his face against the buttocks of a man

████████ to nestling, ████████ to be held in the lap of a man, to kiss him and be petted by him. ████████ ████████ to press his face against the buttocks of men. ████████ to have been associated with his male teachers. ████████ ████████ to the penis. ████████ ████████ to ob- serve the penis. ████████ to masturbation and passive sodomy. ████████ to engage in oral caresses of the penis of his brother-in-law ████████ to ex- perience ████████ to kiss the penis. ████████ ████████ ████████ ████████ ████████ ████████ to act like a man ████████ to get an erection ████████ to penetrate ████ to complete the act ████████ to be satisfied. ████████ to satisfy them. ████████ to discuss his sexual problems with the Lesbian ████████ to make the brother happy. ████████ ████████ y to sacrifice himself ████████ to embrace him, to lie on top of him, to merge with him. ████████ to be like a woman. ████████ ████ to use his mouth to accomplish this ████████ ████████ ████████ ████████ ████████ satisfy ████████ to his sexual desires. ████████

▆▆▆▆▆▆▆▆▆▆▆▆▆▆▆▆▆▆▆▆▆▆ to go on. ▆▆▆▆▆▆ like to be relieved of all sex feelings.

▆▆▆▆▆▆▆▆▆▆▆▆▆▆▆▆▆▆▆▆ to do anything ▆▆▆▆▆▆▆▆▆▆▆▆▆▆▆▆▆▆▆ to be a crash.

After the hospitals, I'd spent many years pretending: either to be younger and more innocent, more oblivious, than I was, or else to be unafraid, or sluttier, or more radical—a *provocateur*—and many times I'd be tripped up, or caught out, and burnt by the exposure.

Juan had taught me to laugh at the past, to laugh at my tendency toward pathos. He modeled a kind of droll humor for me, back in that other place, us two on a bench, pathetic but giggling.

Still, in moments, speaking with Juan there in the Palace, I'd be reminded of the false self, the pseudophilosophical self, or the naif, or simply remember, in a flash, a scene in a bar, or in bed with some man, and what a phony I'd been, or how afraid, or repulsed; how I grasped desperately for admiration, or pity, and lied to get it, and I'd burn all over again, with embarrassment, and find myself unable to go on.

"Sometimes, with you, I think, *It's not me.*"

"Not you, nene?"

"I think, *I'd like to be sincere.*"

"Gosh. Why?"

"It's just that, while we were speaking just now, I suddenly felt foolish. I had this memory of making a fool of myself, and I felt the shame, as hot as ever, or worse, because it's you, Juan."

"Tell me."

"It's trivial, really. I'm in a bar with an older man I'm trying to pick up. I come up with some lame line about provocation and pleasure, and I kind of coo the words. I'm nineteen, and new to hustling, new to flirting even, and the man looks at me with . . . I don't know . . . sympathy, but also . . ."

"Incredulity?"

"Yes. As if he's a director and I'm auditioning for the role of some Depression-era Hollywood vamp. And failing the audition."

"What did you say, exactly?"

"Something along the lines of, *I prefer provocation to pleasure.*"

"And how did he respond?"

"I remember. He says, *Probably you just confuse the two.* Then pats my hand and turns his back to me."

"I like the sound of this man."

"Juan, do you know who is responsible for the erasures? Or what the hidden text says?"

"I might. I probably don't."

"You enjoy frustrating me."

"Not provoking? Pleasing?"

"Forget it."

"Darling, the only thing anyone should be embarrassed about is taking themselves too seriously. Anyway, isn't that what mystery is? Your blackouts, these erasures? Frustration as art?"

" cried Manuelito happily.

Juan was dying, but only in the light, and only in the body. In the dark, his voice filled the room, sharper and more alive than I.

Each day, before the sun rose, in the short glow of daybreak, the desert light came blue and bright and gentle and I would part the curtains while Juan slept and look at death, a pile on the mattress. I knew the same body was once very beautiful, a feminine boy-child with long eyelashes. Juan had served as model to a children's book illustrator and kept a torn page taped to the wall by the bed: a rendering of him as a doe-eyed innocent. I would look at the illustration and then at Juan corpselike on the bed, and I could not reconcile the two images in my mind. Soon the sun crept over the ledge, pierced into the room, and it was time, once again, to draw the shade, pull closed the curtains, and shut out the heat.

While Juan slept, I moved out into the hallway, carrying the day's trash, which I dropped into a chute built into the wall. All the doors to the other rooms were shut, no sounds or signs of life, so I was surprised when a man strode out of the bathroom—strode in my direction—bare-chested, moist, a thin white towel outlining the soft bulge of his cock. I was reminded of the sex clubs I'd stalked back in the city, and just like in those places, the man gave me a solemn nod as he passed, a greeting, which could also have been an invitation. I followed him into his room and got down on my knees and took him into my mouth, but only for a moment, before he slid his hands into my armpits and lifted me to standing, getting down onto his own knees, and I closed my eyes and came quickly. We never said a word; I didn't even notice whether he had finished himself or not; I didn't look for evidence, but selfishly scurried out, pushing my penis back into my underwear. He could have been thirty, or fifty, or a ghost.

When I returned, Juan, wakened, faced the wall, head propped on an elbow, picking at the wallpaper. He motioned for me to come and look at the seal he'd uncovered, or a sea lion perhaps, balancing a striped beach ball on its nose. He smelled rank, vinegary; for several days, I'd been thinking about how to broach the topic of a bath.

N ene, do you sleep?"

"Never, Juan."

"Where are you, just now, who are you with?"

"The landlady. I'm on my way out the door for good, never to return to that house. I stop before the French doors that separate her living room from the main hall. The doors are glass, uncurtained. I can both see and hear her on the other side, praying at her little altar, with the candles and the mirror, and all around are taped pictures of saints, and photographs of children and grandchildren, and her own parents, I presume, in black and white, and the old island pictures she's salvaged from the wreckage. She doesn't turn to see me, doesn't know I'm there, but I can see her face in the reflection, round and full with forgiveness. I'm amazed how quickly she's released her anger over the flood. Those of my belongings not destroyed by water damage she's had boxed up and brought down to the basement, so repairs can get underway; repairs that will take some time, and all the while the place will remain unrentable. I hear her say, *Where will you go?* But no one is around; she's alone. She says, *Should I worry about you?* I want to believe she's speaking to me, and I think it's the kindest way to phrase that question. *I don't know,* I want to say, *please don't worry about me.* But I do not go in to her. I stay outside the door; I say nothing."

"A few weeks before the flood, she had stopped me, there in the main hall, as I was on my way out on some errand, or to meet some man from the internet, and she had held out a gift bag, telling me they were little things, trinkets, which she'd picked up for me on her last trip home, but had forgotten till then to give. A key chain in the shape of a palm tree, and a coffee mug that read SOMEONE IN PUERTO RICO LOVES ME. Already by that time, I was having a hard time focusing. I didn't quite know what to say. I looked at the mug, at her face, her mug, at the empty key ring. Speechless. *Why don't I take them up for you*, she said, nodding her head in the direction of the second floor. *I'll put them there, just outside your door.* And so I handed the gifts back."

"How about you tell me one thing about your mother."

"Now?"

"For context."

"But we keep going backward."

"Please. Just one thing. Make it terrible."

My mother was a screamer. Nervous, terrified, prone to panic. Though when I picture her screaming, what I see and hear in my mind is a vision from a time well before I was born. She first told me the story when I was kid, very young—a vivid scene that's stayed with me, always. She would often tell me things; she'd pull herself away, to a shoebox in the back of the closet filled with photos from the fifties and sixties and seventies. (*The white borders, the scalloped edges. I don't know why they ever stopped printing photos like that, do you, Juan? If everything stayed the same, you wouldn't have cause for your precious nostalgia, nene.*) My mother exerted an immense gravitational force when she retreated, to the floor of the closet, cradling the shoebox. I don't think she ever beckoned me, she didn't have to, I just knew to come and sit and wait for a story. All the stories amazed me—I'd never really been outside the neighborhood, whereas she seemed to have roamed the earth when just a girl, fifteen, pregnant. I wouldn't have been surprised if she'd told me she birthed my brother all alone in a prairie barn, propped up against a bale of hay, among the soft neighing of horses. Or in a manger, I suppose. This was that reverential age when no woman compared in beauty, or mystery, not even the Virgin.

ROSE S.*

General impression:
Any description of Rose would be ▮▮▮▮▮▮▮▮▮▮▮▮▮▮▮▮
▮▮▮▮▮▮▮▮▮▮▮▮▮▮▮▮▮▮▮▮▮▮▮▮▮▮▮▮▮▮▮▮▮▮▮▮▮▮▮
▮▮▮▮▮▮▮▮▮▮▮▮▮▮▮▮▮▮▮▮▮▮▮▮▮▮▮ a ▮▮▮▮▮▮▮▮▮▮
▮▮▮▮▮▮▮▮▮▮▮▮▮▮▮▮▮▮▮▮▮▮▮▮▮▮▮▮▮▮▮▮▮▮▮▮▮▮▮
▮▮▮▮▮▮ Rose ▮▮▮▮▮▮▮▮▮▮▮▮▮▮▮▮▮▮▮▮▮▮▮▮▮▮▮
▮▮▮▮▮▮▮▮▮▮▮▮▮▮▮▮▮▮▮▮▮▮▮▮▮▮▮▮▮▮▮▮▮▮▮▮▮▮▮
▮▮▮▮▮▮▮▮▮▮▮▮▮▮▮▮▮▮▮▮▮▮▮▮▮▮▮▮▮▮▮▮▮▮▮▮▮▮▮
▮▮▮▮▮▮ prolong her vowels ▮▮▮▮▮▮▮▮▮▮▮▮▮▮▮▮
▮▮▮▮▮▮▮▮▮▮▮▮▮▮ hesitate ▮▮▮▮▮▮▮▮▮▮▮▮▮▮▮
▮▮▮▮▮▮▮ describe ▮ a statue ▮▮▮▮▮▮▮▮▮▮▮▮▮
▮▮▮▮▮▮ white, translucent skin. ▮▮▮▮▮▮▮▮▮▮▮
▮▮▮▮▮▮▮▮▮▮▮▮▮▮▮▮▮▮▮▮▮ make her ▮▮▮ a
▮▮ Rubens ▮▮▮▮▮▮▮▮▮▮▮▮▮ paint ▮▮▮▮▮▮▮▮
▮▮▮▮▮▮▮▮▮▮▮▮▮ her dreamy blue eyes ▮▮▮▮
shrewd and penetrating and ▮▮ low, ▮▮▮▮▮▮▮▮▮
▮▮▮▮▮▮▮▮▮▮▮▮▮▮▮▮▮▮▮▮▮▮▮▮▮▮▮▮▮▮▮▮▮▮▮▮▮
Rose ▮▮▮▮▮▮▮▮▮▮▮▮▮▮▮▮▮▮▮▮▮▮▮▮▮▮▮▮▮▮▮▮
▮▮▮▮▮▮▮▮▮▮▮▮▮▮▮▮▮▮▮▮▮▮▮▮▮▮▮▮ is still
▮▮▮▮▮▮▮▮▮▮▮▮▮▮▮▮▮▮▮▮▮▮▮▮▮▮▮▮▮▮▮▮▮▮▮▮
▮▮▮▮▮▮▮▮▮▮▮▮▮▮▮▮▮▮▮▮▮▮▮▮▮▮▮▮▮▮▮▮▮▮▮▮▮
▮▮▮▮▮▮▮▮▮▮▮▮▮▮▮ a ▮▮▮▮ Rose ▮▮▮▮▮▮▮▮▮
▮▮▮▮▮▮▮▮▮▮▮▮▮▮▮▮▮▮▮▮▮▮▮▮▮▮▮▮ a ▮▮▮ tangible return.
▮▮▮▮▮▮▮▮▮▮▮▮▮

919

My father joined the air force, just a kid really. He came of legal age right after the draft ended; no more troops were being sent to Vietnam. He was lucky that way. They sent him to North Dakota, to the badlands. My mother cried and knitted and pined. Back in Brooklyn, she was locked up in a home for unwed pregnant teens. Catholic. Austere nuns. He'd fled from the responsibility, but my mother manufactured within him a change of heart, through letters posted to his base, and one day, he sent for her to come join him. He must have been lonely. Or remorseful. Or perhaps he'd truly found religion. In his childhood, his own father had converted from Catholicism to Jehovah's Witness after he left my grandmother and remarried, and so my father had a certain familiarity with the sect when, there in Minot, a group of Witnesses got hold of him, converted him. Witnesses don't believe in military service—I don't know how that all worked out. Perhaps he already had his mind on creating a reason for early discharge. At any rate, he sent for my mother and she came, and they married, and she gave birth to my brother, there in Minot. They lived in a trailer park; some of the neighbors were military, but most were Witnesses. My parents fought over God. Physically. Then they would make up, passionately. They were teenagers. (*You can imagine, Juan. Nene, I can imagine.*) They had moved from Brooklyn to Minot. Winter came earlier and colder and harder than they'd ever known. He beat her. Some neighbors called the cops; she was such a screamer. But she wouldn't press charges. Then came the holidays: Thanksgiving she gave up, but she drew the line at Christmas. *My baby was going to have Christmas* was how she put it to me, and she somehow got a tree while he was gone, a tiny little thing, dragged it inside, put it up, trimmed the tree with yarn and paper cutouts, whatever she could find, a pair of earrings. For the baby to look at. But Witnesses do not celebrate, and when he came home, they fought, and he hit, and she screamed and screamed, and the cops came again, and this time one cop pulled her aside and he said to her, *Little girl, what are you doing here?*

Ma always cried at that point in the story, in her closet, she'd cry. I'd hear this story again and again, and she'd always cry at the same point in the same story. *I'll never forget what he said to me. Little girl, what are you doing here?*"

"A fair enough question, considering."

"Do you know, Juan, for years, I carried that cop around in my head?"

"The imago."

"I don't know that word. I don't know what you're saying."

"Jung. Or Lacan. You know, if I were an analyst, you'd be paying through the nose for these chats."

"Am I not paying enough, Juan?"

"How do you mean you carried him? What did he look like, this cop?"

"I don't know. Handsome, tall, mustachioed, but beyond that I suppose a kind of blankness, just the mouth and lips and moustache, the rest shadowed by the brim of his hat, western style, a cop's hat, stripes running down the legs of his pants, tight at the crotch, boots, gloves. *Little girl,* he says, so gently. My mother told me that he took the baby in his own arms and sent her inside to pack a bag, put her in the back of the car, handed back the baby, and drove her all the way out to the airport, where he bought her a plane ticket back home, to Brooklyn. He gave her a little money, too, just to have in her pocket. I tried asking all kinds of questions about the cop: Did he ever call to check in, to see how she was doing? How did she thank him? I wanted to find him, I suppose. But my mother brushed aside such questions; the point was definitely not the cop—she wasn't interested in cops—it was the phrase, *Little girl, what are you doing here?* It had terrified her. Broken her. She'd survived the nuns, her parents' expulsion, childbirth, my father's conversion; she'd kept her baby fed and healthy, knitted booties and blankets, learned to make her own baby food by steaming and mashing frozen vegetables, by minding her peas and carrots; she'd held off all the terror, by talking to my brother, growing inside her, and then by looking at his face; and she'd thought that maybe she was a mother now, and not a little girl."

"She hadn't dared to ask herself that question—*what am I doing here?*"

"Yes, that's right. I see that now. I also see that the cop—well, who knows his motivations—Minot, North Dakota, in the seventies, these teenagers, this Puerto Rican guy, this petite white girl, who knows, who knows? I was a teenager myself by the time it occurred to me to ask if the cop's intervention was tinged with racism. My mother shrugged; she couldn't believe I'd held on to the story. She tried to get me to understand how naive she was at that time, how much she loved my father, and he loved her. As a child, I was too thick to understand that my mother was not looking for a hero, or savior, or father figure, or law and order. She wanted my father to be a father to their child, a husband, to stop hitting her, all of which, after many years, she would achieve. Together, they pulled themselves, and us boys, out of the hole."

"You sound proud, nene."

"I mean, they were smart. I could talk and talk about them, and never get it right, the complication. They were both so constantly inconsistent. Both ninth-grade dropouts, though hyper-intelligent, literary-minded. I don't mean to say that our home was filled with books—it wasn't—but stories, empathic connections with the downtrodden and the villainous. Both manipulators of narrative; they shared an absurdist sense of humor about the human condition, about our own family's bad luck. I couldn't see any of that then; what I could see was that they were very often not in control. I couldn't understand that, back there in Minot, my mother had not wanted to be saved, because as a child, in that home, I very much wanted to be saved. He may have stopped hitting her, but not us, and my eldest brother, especially, as he pushed into adolescent rebellion, was beat down hard. Probably, in reality, that cop was not handsome; I think my mother would have said, would have noticed if he were. And there are so many ways to inflect that phrase, aren't there, to call someone *little girl*, to ask *what are you doing here?* But in my child's mind, he asked her very kindly, very kindly indeed, with the benevolence, concern, and gentle eroticism one might find in a fairy tale. I looked for him everywhere."

And then, when I was eight or nine or so, my father left for six months, to boot camp, to become a state trooper. His prolonged absence, the career itself, came out of nowhere; we boys were never privy to the deliberations of the adult world. Later, I would learn he had been recruited into the force to work narcotics because he spoke Spanish, because he spoke English with a Brooklyn accent, because of the color of his skin and the kink of his hair, because he knew how to act. Already so strong, he returned home transformed, not only muscled in new ways, but outfitted with high black boots that came up over the calf, and a felt Stetson hat with a purple ribbon; armed. Suddenly there were cops in our house all the time, drinking, cursing, shouting, their feet up on the coffee table. My father's new social world. None had arrived to save me, to call me *little boy*, to ask what I was doing here. *Pigs*, my mother hissed. It was the first time I heard the slur; I thought she'd made it up.

Later still, much later, I would overhear my father on the phone, speaking with regret about the arrest of a young mother, a dealer's girlfriend, whom he'd befriended over a yearlong sting—a woman pressured into the trade herself, then swept up in the eventual bust. I heard him detail what might happen next, with the children, and the pain in his voice. Then he switched to Spanish, and I knew he was speaking to his partner, Hector, a gregarious man who, when he came by for dinner, would often wink at me after a lewd joke or a teasing jab about my father's good looks, as if we were complicit in the important work of keeping my father grounded. I loved Hector for that, though late at night, after many beers, the joking would sometimes cease, and they would speak about work, always in Spanish, excluding me, but allowing me to notice other things: how deeply each searched the eyes of the other; how if one raised an eyebrow, the other might flick a dismissive hand. I noticed the passion with which one insisted on a point and the deadly seriousness with which the other listened. I had been told that the work they did was very dangerous, and I worried my father might be discovered, and stabbed, or shot. But watching them drink together, I came to feel the danger may be more insidious, or that it had already arrived. I felt—in an unformed, childish way, outside of any political framework—not just that they might be hurt, but that they were *being* hurt by what they called "the job."

In the desert, in the Palace, I lost track of time, not just of the hours and dates, but also of a certain sense of the temporal, the march of single day. Back in the old life, the rhythm of my days had to do with being broke, trying to hustle up some money, or worrying over the absence of money, or distracting myself from the worry. But here in the village, everything sold for dirt cheap. I could afford smokes, could afford a drink. I paid no rent. The little I'd collected from bus station hand jobs and some light cocksucking seemed to stretch and stretch. Yet the habits of poverty run deep—and I felt, underneath the surface, the same old dread. A constant sense that I'd forgotten to attend to a vague but terrible urgency. I'd startle out from under some half dream, some reverie of the old life, and think: *Oh God, what's coming?* Perhaps I actually spoke the words aloud on occasion, because Juan would sometimes answer, in a soothing and assured voice: *Nothing, nene. Only your nothingness.* And I'd slip again into that distracted middle place, apart from all anxieties, earthly or otherwise.

As the days became more and more indistinguishable, I grew lethargic; in the heat, I hardly needed meals, hardly felt any hunger. Soon enough, I ventured out only after the sun dipped below the horizon, and not for long, just down to the corner store to pick up a can or two of soup for Juan, sometimes a cold beer for myself, and every night a tamale, which the proprietress kept piled in a metal tub on the counter by the register, under a heat lamp. She would peel back the husk, ladle over the salsa verde, stab a plastic fork straight down into the heart of the masa, and hand

the tamale over to me. Neither of us spoke a word, in either language; we communicated through gesture, and the entire ritual
reminded me of an old black-and-white movie I'd seen—voodoo
exploitation: the unwrapping of a little doll child, the stabbing,
the silence.

II

THE VARIANTS

More often . . . the urge to document and the urge to disappear, though contradictory, are fused.

—**HEATHER LOVE**, *Underdogs*

Y ou've got to give me something. Please, tell me one thing you've learned, Juan, about these two volumes."

"Ha. The facts of life? The truth about *MEN* and *WOMEN*?"

"Please, Juan."

"All right, then, nene. But only to reward your admirable impatience."

FOREWORD

The Committee for the Study of Sex Variants was founded in the spring of 1935.

touching embracing

concerning

punitive

inadequate

this monograph has been

from its beginning. embodied

by a group of sex variants, voluntary

v

They came to advocate, to inform, to protest the raids and roundups; they came out of curiosity; they came on a lark, for a bit of a hoot, and found themselves intrigued; they came as a favor; some arrived angry, righteous; others confused and suicidal; more than a few came with desperate hope for a cure. Those who stormed out often returned. They learned something of their own desire. They were asked to remember, and they remembered: a glimpse of the father in the shower; being discovered with the neighbor girl; an awful licking; the days before the advent of nylon, and how the silk hosiery rolled gently down to the ankle; they remembered children whose custody they'd lost; they remembered children they'd abandoned. And when they were asked to strip, they obliged, and their names were anonymized, and their faces blurred, until they were confined to the realm of the symbolic, naked and labeled: Narcissistic, Homosexual, Hoodlum— determined and erased.

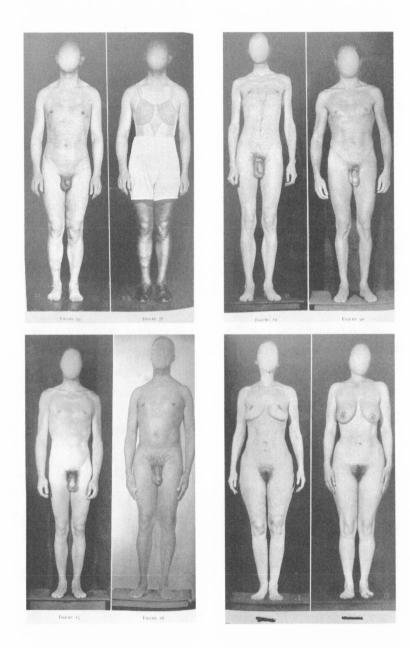

Dr. George W. Henry served as the lead researcher, chair of the committee, and so his name alone graced the cover of the *Sex Variants* books. In reality, the project began with Jan Gay, many years before Henry arrived on the scene. And even after the committee took over, Jan remained integral to the study, personally rounding up the volunteers. Some were friends, or friends of friends, and some she approached in the usual bars and haunts.

The study was first published in 1941, but research began in earnest in 1935. As the years passed, the study rippled out into ever-widening circles of queer sociability, touching the various ethnicities of the New York scene: the Italians, the Irish, the Blacks, the Cubans, the Poles, the Jews, the Anglos, the rich and the poor. The times were hard—the Great Depression—the volunteers Jan rounded up skewed slightly toward the middle and lower classes, and skewed, too, toward artistic types, rather than industrial laborers or service workers. Many volunteers dragged in a lover to be examined, or an ex, or a sibling who also happened to be sissy or butch.

A wealthy man (or rather, a man who had come from great wealth, and come out, and thus been disinherited) persuaded several of the hustlers he frequented to make themselves available. His name was Thomas Painter, and the more he recruited volunteers into the study, the more he became an influential fixture. He was, like Jan, an amateur researcher, though his research interest was personal, physical, taking notes on the straight hustlers, the studs, who made themselves available to the queens; eventually taking notes on every one of his sexual encounters.

After the committee finished its work and published the two volumes, and after the war ended, and on through the postwar years and into the fifties—during the great waves of Boricua migration to New York—Thomas Painter developed a particular admiration for Puerto Ricans. He traveled to the island many times, conducting research, hands-on, lips-on research, which he hoped one day to have published. He referred to the 1950s as his Puerto Rican years.

"And you knew them both?"

"Who's telling this story?"

"How strange, Juan."

"Jan I knew when I was just a child; I met her through her then-wife, Zhenya. For a very brief time, I was handed into their care: my chaperones when I was sent north, to New York. And then many years later, when I was grown, I knew Thom."

"Try to tell it in order. Don't skip ahead."

"Thom would sometimes speak of the work he'd done on the committee, and the woman he'd worked with there—a nudist, a bulldagger, pleasant enough when she was clothed and not drunk. He'd tell funny stories about her, slightly cruel. I never knew at that time he was speaking of Jan. I only realized much later, pieced it together after the book came into my life and I saw her name, a single perfunctory acknowledgment in the introduction, for services rendered."

JAN GAY

J an was born in 1902, to a midwestern family, and came out as
gay in grand style by the age of twenty. She traveled to Europe and studied with the famed sexologist Magnus Hirschfeld,
before the Nazis sacked his institute and burned the books. With
Zhenya, she founded a nudist colony in upstate New York; she
wrote a book, *On Going Naked*, about the history of naturalist
movements in the US and Europe—a sensation, not least because
of the photographic inserts of men and women, unclothed, and
Zhenya's hand-drawn illustrations. For the book's documentary
film adaptation, *This Nude World*, Jan wrote the script.

While traveling around Europe, from Berlin to Paris, London
to Oxford, Jan had begun, as a side project, research into lesbian
lives, taking interviews and sexual histories from over three hundred women, a moderated version of the Hirschfeld technique,
which she collected into a manuscript. Her failure to find a publisher willing to take on the risqué topic without the cover of a
medical expert was the inciting incident that eventually led to the
formation of the Committee for the Study of Sex Variants. Jan's
amateur research formed the basis, the germ, of all to come.

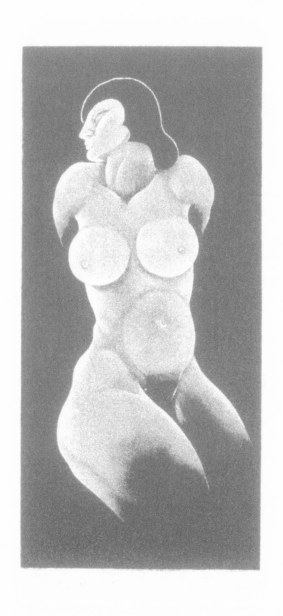

J uan had tracked down the documentary and read the book, *On Going Naked*, though not until he was grown, decades after he had known Jan and Zhenya. What he found most re- markable was not so much the nudist history contained therein, but the two possible visions of modern Europe on display. The book was published in 1932, and the film was seem- ingly pieced together from stock footage of nudist colonies in France and Germany in the late 1920s and early 1930s. With the power of hindsight, Juan saw glimpses of the nascent fascism everywhere in the nudist camps: the cult of fitness, the perfection of the body as an aesthetic form, the emphasis on folk traditions and sport, the youth clubs. But so, too, he glimpsed a competing anarchic spirit: the collective vision of shared re- sources. Colonies set up by and for the poor and working classes focused more on communion with one another and with nature; they were places where one could be fed for little or no money, places unconcerned with notions of idealized athleticism.

Juan himself claimed to be an anarchist. His conception of anar- chism was a kind of faith, a spiritual practice. He was never very politically active, though he greatly admired the Puerto Rican so- cialists in New York, especially Jesús Colón, whose weekly column in the *Daily Worker* he followed religiously. He told me Colón's story: How in 1917, when he was just sixteen, he left Puerto Rico as a stowaway tucked into the linen closet of a passenger ship and arrived in New York penniless; how it was important to remem- ber that the "father" of the Nuyoricans, the first great chronicler of the Puerto Rican experience in English, was Black and socialist; and how he committed his life to his people, Puerto Ricans, and Black people more broadly, and to the working man everywhere. Colón joined the Communist Party, was hauled before the Housing Un-American Activities Committee—and refused to recant. Juan found himself incapable of joining parties, but appreciated Colón's approach to dismantling racism and capitalism, which was through story, humor, and humanism; through writing. He wrote in vignettes, each a slice of life—the evocation of a single moment—and in this way, avoided the error of dogma and grand narratives. Each vignette, Juan said, was a kind of meditation, offering new ways of seeing and relating.

"Jesús and Jan were born just months apart. How about that, nene?"

"You must have known him—or met him at some point?"

"Youth with its enthusiasm saw to it that neither the fire nor the singing would die out. That's Colón. I am delivering his message to you, from across time."

"To keep on singing?"

"And burning, nene."

"And Jan's original research, have you seen it?"

"Nothing remains. No trace."

"Lost to history?"

"Deliberately trashed. And not by Jan. You see, this committee, which was made up of a number of doctors and professionals in various disciplines—psychiatrists, parapsychologists, gynecologists and maternal health specialists, a chemist, the director of Bellevue, the former commissioner of the NYC Department of Corrections—absorbed everything they needed of Jan's research into the study and never returned the manuscript to her. They tried to hold on to Thom's research as well, but he threw such a fit, threatening a lawsuit and generally raising hell, that they handed his materials back at the end of the study. He went on to work with Kinsey, whom he found more amenable to the approach of an experiential documentarian."

"By *experiential*, you mean he wrote about guys he paid to fuck him?"

"It's true, all erotic experience can be reduced to crudeness, nene. But does that mean it ought to be?"

"And you, Juan? You were one of his . . . lovers?"

"The point is the committee didn't want its findings to be tainted by Thomas's theories, or Jan's activist approach to documenting lesbian lives. The committee's focus was pathology, mixing the newish Freudian psychosexual theories with physiological explanations for deviance. Eugenics."

"I will go to the bank by
the wood
and become undisguised
and naked,
I am mad for it to be in
contact with me."

Story by
JAN GAY

Author of
"ON GOING NAKED"

Dr. Henry personally chose which variants to include in the final published study. The committee interviewed hundreds of variants but only published case studies of eighty—forty men and forty women who were, Henry said, particularly informative in their interviews. Forty men and forty women. Forty days and forty nights. His was an era more uniformly literate in biblical metaphor; the reference would have been clear. *Forty and forty* is a kind of shorthand, a catchall, for a time of trial and tribulation. The forty days and forty nights of Moses fasting in the desert. Of Moses receiving God's law on Mount Sinai. Of Jesus, fasting in the desert."

"The flood, too, right? It rained for forty nights and forty days?"

"The time span of purification. And in Sodom, too, when Abraham begs God to spare the city, the Lord cuts a deal. He says to Abraham, *If I find in Sodom fifty righteous within the city, then I will spare all the place for their sakes.* But Abraham haggles. *Peradventure there shall lack five of the fifty righteous: wilt thou destroy all the city for lack of five?* So God goes down to forty-five, but Abraham pushes on: Well, in that case, how about forty? And the Lord agrees he will not destroy the city, *for forty's sake.*"

"God, Juan, how do you know all this?"

"It's Sodom, darling, worth committing to memory. *Behold now, I have taken upon me to speak unto the Lord, which am but dust and ashes* . . . Sadly, the phrase *bargaining with God* has come to be a universal cliché, a stage of grief. But here is Abraham, literally haggling. A lovely scene. And I love, too, the word *peradven-*

ture. English was at its best in the time of King James, don't you think?"

"I really wouldn't know."

"Well, you'll have to trust me. Anyway, the point, I suppose, is that, for me, *Sex Variants* contains the testimonies of the righteous, forty men and forty women who might save us all from the hellfires; perverts, presented in all their glory."

"Have you seen a copy of the book without the blackouts?"

"I have, once, briefly. I had to order it to be specially delivered to the library and was not allowed to take it off the premises. The librarian stood watching me as I read, and nene, she watched with distaste. Though I prefer our copy here, I prefer the books just as I found them, covered in black. Filled with little poems of illumination. A counternarrative to whatever might have been Dr. Henry's agenda. No particular benefit to reading in order. Flip through to any page and there is a sketch of a life, ever unfolding, rising up out of the past, each a single testimony of how that person did or did not get over."

I don't make the effort. ▮▮▮▮▮▮▮▮▮▮▮▮▮▮

▮▮▮▮▮▮▮▮▮. Under the skin ▮▮▮▮▮▮▮▮

▮▮▮▮ masculine pride. ▮▮▮▮▮▮▮▮▮▮ a perverted maternal complex. I don't like babies ▮▮ they are very tiny, like bugs. ▮▮▮▮▮▮ I am more ▮▮▮▮▮▮ than the average Lesbian. ▮▮▮▮▮▮▮▮

I never ▮ sleep ▮▮▮▮▮▮▮▮▮▮▮▮

I love ▮▮▮▮▮▮ Turkish baths, the steam and confusion, the horrible-looking bodies ▮▮▮▮▮▮▮▮▮▮ cheap wine and harlots. ▮▮▮▮▮▮▮▮ It feels good to have my stomach massaged.

When people talk about homosexual geniuses I think ▮▮▮▮▮

▮▮▮▮▮▮▮▮ everybody under the table ▮▮▮▮▮▮▮▮▮▮ I take a teaspoonful of beer ▮▮▮▮▮▮ sink▮ through the earth. ▮▮▮▮▮ I can't sleep ▮▮▮▮▮▮

▮▮▮▮▮▮▮▮

▮▮▮▮ The other night ▮▮▮▮ I was in an operating room where a peasant woman was having her legs amputated. ▮▮▮▮▮▮ pleasant ▮▮▮ women. ▮▮▮▮

▮▮▮▮ might solve my economic problems ▮▮▮

I have a fear of ▮▮▮▮ sleep and a fear of ▮▮▮▮ After

I lied to you, the other night."

"What lie?"

"Abraham actually haggles the Lord down, past forty, all the way to ten. But forty was more convenient, eh, niño? For the story I was spinning?"

"Either way, it's hilarious. *Find me ten righteous Sodomites in all the city, and I will not destroy it.* It's like a joke in search of a punch line."

"Lord, I've been waiting all my life for just one."

"Lord, a good fag is hard to find."

"Vulgarity, nene."

"Sodom: A Disco Inferno."

"¡Basta! . . . Remember my poor bladder . . . the mattress . . ."

Each day, Juan's naps stretched longer, deeper, more vehement. I watched over him, and I noticed the little signs of a great confrontation, a long and hard-fought battle unfolding in his dreams. He ground his teeth and furrowed his eyebrows; he balled his fists and grasped at the sheets; he chirped and he moaned. In the room, the movements and sounds played on a minor scale, but I knew that on the other side, in the dreamworld, a terrible orchestra blew the horns and clashed the symbols, while Juan wrestled some faceless monster, vicious and sublime, like Jacob hoping to pin the angel and extract the blessing. And I knew that Juan would lose.

Nothing roused him. I could be as noisy as I pleased, and sometimes I sang aloud to distract myself from the miserable struggling. I almost never saw his eyes anymore; he slept through the days, and at night we sat in near total darkness. Juan could no longer tolerate the bedside lamp, nor could he tolerate me in the bed beside him. If I needed to see, to fix his soup, or if I wanted to read, I would crack the door and allow in a sliver of light from the hall. Still, in the dark, in the night, he came alive, a disembodied voice, full with Juan's gentle spirit and humor. During the day, I read and reread the books, the erasures. I wondered what I ought to be looking for in those testimonies. Solace? Strategy? Juan himself? But when I asked if he'd perhaps been one of the subjects of the study, he only laughed.

"Me? Certainly not. Do the math. I'd be long dead."

"Sorry, Juan."

"I'm not dead, am I?"

"Not dead, Juan."

"And you—do you live, or are you a ghost? Eh, little boy? What are you doing here?"

During the days, the street outside the window lay quiet, no cars passed, and the sun-baked sidewalks stood empty. In the evenings, a few souls emerged, and we might hear a man whistle to a dog, or the sounds of two passersby in conversation, though never loud enough to catch the words, only a laugh, or a little exclamation of surprise. Until one evening, when there came a handful of voices and shufflings—the sounds of the living—which rose, incrementally, into the unmistakable bustle of a gathered crowd, such as neither of us had heard in the town before. Juan dispatched me to the window to describe for him the scene below.

The first figure I could make out was the woman from the bodega, dressed in the old style, wearing a mantilla. She stood near the center of the group, flattening the thick fabric of her chintz dress, a funereal pattern, in black and shades of purple. I then noticed some of the others were dressed oddly as well, costumed. The bodega woman grabbed a basket of paper flowers and stepped onto a raised platform, which had been erected in the middle of the street and which faced our building. The dozens gathered around the stage fell silent. The woman raised her eyes to the sky. I feared she'd see me, even though I knew that I did nothing wrong by standing and watching the street. She looked into the windows of the Palace, solicitous. *Flores* . . . she called. *Flores para los muertos*. She kept on repeating the phrase, drawing out the *o* sound.

Louder! demanded another woman, a voice in the crowd, I couldn't tell whose. The bodega woman raised the volume, and as

she did so, she also slowed her pace, adding more weariness to her voice. *Flores . . . Flores para los muertos . . .*

"You look as if you're about to be dragged off to meet Pateco, the gravedigger."

"It's terrible, Juan."

"But don't you recognize the scene? Tennessee Williams. *They told me to take the streetcar named Desire, and transfer to one called Cemeteries . . . and get off at Elysian Fields.* They must be rehearsing, nene. That's all. Come away from the window now."

"I know her, the flower seller."

"Of course you do. Come away from the window before she sees you and lures you into some macabre production. Come, come. I'll tell you a story . . . Ah, you forgot to close the curtains."

Mira. I spent a lot of time in this room, slowly withdrawing from the old life. And I read. The library had not yet been shuttered, and once upon a time a bookstore even operated in this ghost town, believe it or not, and so I'd shuffle between the two in search of collections—stories and poetry. I'd lost patience for novels. I did not want to die in the middle of a novel. I wanted only endings, last lines, goodbyes, and reunions. I wondered how might things end for me; how would it read, the final sentence of my life? The verdict?"

"I think you'll live much longer, now that I'm here."

"Oh? I suppose you would think that. One can't help but think all sorts of rubbish sometimes . . . But listen: One day I read a short story, by a writer of whom I'd never heard. Her stories had only recently come to light, posthumously, decades after she'd written them. Collins, the name was. Anyway, the main character in the story I'm thinking of was also very isolated—a woman, an intellectual, or an artist, I can't remember now, but she was beautiful, worldly, long-suffering. Maybe a little mad. A pioneering woman. You know, nene, in my time, we all prayed to our private idols, some famous woman, usually an actress; we memorized her lines, her looks, practiced throwing ourselves down onto the divan, overcome—all of us old-school sissies, we carried these women inside, or alongside, our consciousness, private icons, whose mannerisms and wit we'd call forth . . . mimesis, *Dionysian imitatio* . . . though I suppose that kind of thing has gone out of style."

"What, like Greta Garbo?"

"Like La Lupe. Like Lena Horne . . . Anyway, in the story, the woman is very much alone, and, just as I was doing then, she compulsively reads everything she can get her hands on. Though she reads more methodically than I, moving from genre to genre. Like Goldilocks with the porridges, although nothing satiates; nothing breaches the seclusion. Just when she feels she's reached the nadir of her loneliness, she turns to reading memoirs. *It was one of my finer moments when I discovered that no human life escapes the tribulation of solitude*, she says. *Other souls had suffered such extremes of separation and abandon, and in their wit and irony and quaint homiletic posturing I momentarily lifted myself out of myself and onto a plane of spiritual lamentation.* And I knew then, what I'd been searching for; I wanted to feel that. Outside myself. Lifted."

"Really, Juan, how have you memorized so many passages?"

"Well, I've never seen it put any better. *Quaint homiletic posturing.*"

"And what happens next?"

"The woman—yes, I remember now, she's a musician—she accidentally burns down her house."

"You're kidding."

"Why kidding?"

"Well, it's like the flood, the flood that brought me here."

"Oh? I thought this was a story about me, not you."

Juan found the *Sex Variants* books in a cardboard box full of unwanted belongings, set out in the lobby of the Palace, near the foot of the stairs. On the box flap, in black marker, rather than FREE, or the imploring TAKE ME, someone had written: I'M YOURS NOW. Juan chuckled at the campiness of it all. He could just picture the lonesome soul who wrote the words. He rummaged through, found the two volumes, carried them upstairs, back to his room, to his own solitude, and he read, and reread, what was left of the testimonies of the variants. (*For such a long time I read. Only God knows how long.*) The clever, absurd, and frank ways the variants' stories had been erased, and what remained of their suffering, and hope, and sexual desires; the vernacular and the idioms they used; the vocabulary of the underground 1930s—this queer world that had existed just before his own, or rather, the world into which Juan had been born, and whose attitudes had bled into Juan's own adolescence; the particularities of their sorrow, their persecution; and to see, too, the ways in which they'd been freer and more fluid when it came to sex acts, roles, identities; to be reminded of a time when much had yet to be defined; for a long while, all of this brought not comfort, exactly, but lifted Juan out of himself.

"On to . . . what was it? That place of . . ."

"The plane of spiritual lamentation."

"And is that where we are now?"

[99]

"Did you notice, nene, that when you arrived, the days short-ened and the nights, the darkness, stretched. The cold?"

"No, Juan, it was the start of summer."

"The air changed."

██

██

████████████████████████████████

██ I have not
been without imaginings ████████████████████████
█████ carnal. █████████████ unimaginable. █████████
████████████████████ imagining ████████████████████

At times I have been compared in appearance to Christ. ███████ the
same serenity of expression. ████████████████████████
███████████████████████████████████████ the fine
quality which we associate with womanhood ████████████████

████ Christ-like ██████████████████████████████
█████████████ I was brought ██████████████ from Palestine to
███████████████████ a rosary. █████████████ a number of knots
in a string. ████████████████ I would attempt to pray with that
rosary. █████ in a chair █████████ the rosary in my hands ███████
█████████████████████████████. Outside was
sunshine, trees, flowers, warmth. ████████████████████
███████████ nothing discordant ██████████ I felt transported beyond
the mundane. ██████████████ heightened by prayer. ███████

██

██████████ a physiological state. ████████████████████
███████████████████████████████ a serene situation. ████
██████████████████████ when I was ██████

██ desirous
but not understanding. ███████████████████████████

████████████████████████ Those terrible years when I
had so much trouble ████████████ when I was without a confidante.
When I ████ lost courage ████████████████████████

█████████████████████████ When I had █████████
████████████████ all these abnormalities ████████████
████████ I could tell ██████████████████████████
████ I could tell █████████████████████████
what I wanted ███ this serene situation. ████████████████

L isten. They're gathering again today, Juan. The players."

"You know, in the film version of the play, the Mexican woman who sells the flowers was not Mexican, but Black; a lesbian and a fine actress. Edna Thomas. She played Lady Macbeth in an all-Black production of the Scottish play, only set in Haiti, which came to be known as *Voodoo Macbeth*. A sensation. And she was an acquaintance of Jan and Zhenya's. And one of the variants in the study."

But I'm tired now, of speaking. I'd like to listen a bit."

　　"To me?"

"To you. Dígame. One of your whore stories. Make me laugh."

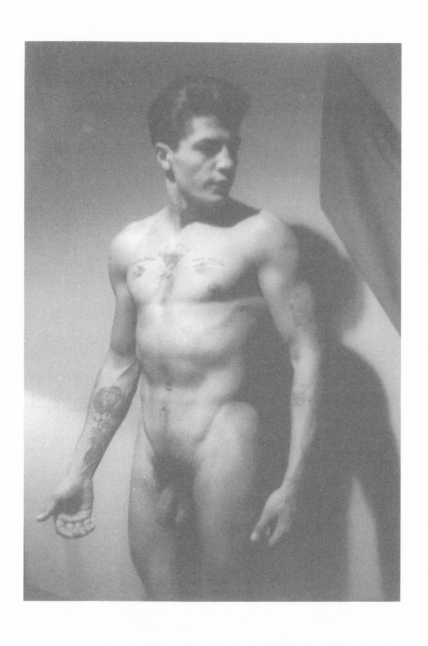

O nce, not so long ago, but far away, I placed an ad on a popular classifieds website under the title *Jack of All Trades, Master of None*. The ad offered to clean, go to the laundromat, organize your bullshit, walk your dog. This was in the personals section, specifically for men seeking men. I was twenty-five, but easily passed for younger—my cheeks were still hairless—so I advertised nineteen. I remember it was autumn, and I remember feeling plagued by an unbearable need for both intimacy and estrangement, for the queerness of touch. Mostly, I placed that ad because I was broke.

I got a lot of responses, enough to waste the afternoon, idly mesmerized by my cascading inbox. Most simply demanded nude photos, in all caps: *SEND PICS*. One respondent stood out, his tone restrained, easy. He required someone to run errands and walk his dog. The exchange of sex was implied in the hourly rate he was willing to pay, but we were both cautious and indirect in our emails. *I feel like I get you*, he wrote. He was silver-haired, white, early fifties, well-preserved. A wealthy narcissist; it wasn't that he got me so much as that there was no one he didn't feel he had. (*Raspberries may be well-preserved, nene, not men. This man was—that one guy from the television show* Mad Men *comes to mind now, but you've probably never even heard of it, huh, Juan? A soap opera set in a lunatic asylum? Worse. Advertising.*)

Here's what I remember of the dog: she spent all day in a crate, even though Mad Man worked from home. She was untrained, destructive. At the sound of my entrance, she freaked, and then at the sight of me she freaked harder, paddling her front paws furiously against the mesh metal door, which made the unlocking only more difficult and extended her agony. She never barked, because she couldn't; she had been bred not to bark, but barks lived inside her, I read them in her face, in the way she opened her mouth and pulsed her vocal cords. A light reddish brown, achingly handsome—she looked healthy, expensive. A basenji. I remember her black eyes, deceptively kind and questioning, and how the skin of her forehead wrinkled to a peak in the middle as she pulled her brows down at the sides. At home, this was her most constant look, one of silent imploring, but when we were alone together a shadow would pass, and her features would harden into rage. She often tried to bite me.

At first, I was appalled at her over-crating, and unsurprised at her neuroses, but after some weeks my compassion waned. One day, Mad Man sent me around the corner with six hundred dollars in cash to buy a leather jacket. For the dog. He lived in the West Village, so the request was neither improbable nor impossible. My rent was four-fifty. I had a bed in a living room in an unhip part of Brooklyn—not the entire room to myself, mind, but a bed stuck in a corner of the communal living room, behind a screen. I walked to that doggy clothier in a fury that transferred from Mad Man to the dog herself. I found myself fantasizing about somehow destroying the dog and walking away with the cash. I ought to have felt solidarity, stuck as we were at the bottom, Mad Man master to us both. Instead, I felt jealous of her tiny, perfect jacket.

I quit and considered getting a legit job. I remember sitting at the kitchen table with my laptop as my friends joked that I should put down on my résumé, under past work, "Being a little bitch." All the sunlight came through the kitchen, so we packed around the table, some up on the counter, drinking shit wine. My friends, these tough women and queers, were all too sharp and creative for their jobs. It seemed as though all the people I had ever known, everyone I was coming up with then, were somehow bending their will to a Mad Man, for the money. We packed into that kitchen to help one another get through the bends—with dark humor, with shouted advice. We bitched about everything. The trick was not to fall into shame, or, worse, quietude.

If I'm nostalgic, it's not because I was happy in those precarious years. But I was deeply moved by our resourcefulness. No rich parents lurked in the background; we kept one another afloat. We drank ourselves messy, and when one spiraled downward, the rest chased after, to help, to mock and make light, to tease that person back to the surface. Always, we waited for money to appear, as if it might pour in on a beam of sunshine. We waited, and, in our waiting, we were loud.

My hunch is that Mad Man gave the dog up. Either that or he finally broke her. Anyway, she's old now, or else she's dead. But I have this fantasy that she's still chewing up the living room, still slamming against the limits of that cage, only now she's vocalized, yapping and howling, and it's a kind of music, and the whole neighborhood can hear her frustration and understand. And the song is a lament, something camp and bluesy, about how there ain't no shame in being a bitch, but, Lord, be a bitch that barks.

Who is it that likens nostalgia to returning to a familiar street only to find the geography has been tampered with? *Half-real, half a rearrangement of the sleeping mind . . .* Something like that. When first I read that line, it struck me as a warning—not to get lost back there, in the misremembered past, that half-dreamt barrio you can't recall how to escape. Eh, niño?"

"But I did make you laugh."

"The dog in the tiny leather jacket. I could just see her, though in my mind's eye she wore sunglasses as well, a little greaser."

Well now there's nothing in nor out o' the world—
Good except truth: yet this, the something else,
What's this then, which proves good yet seems untrue?

One night Juan recounted the entire plot of an epic poem by Robert Browning. How in 1860, in Florence, Browning bought an "old square yellow book" from a street vendor. How he became obsessed with the story he found therein. The book was nearly two centuries old, less a book even and more a collection of materials—pamphlets, legal documents, personal letters—all relating to a sensational trial from the 1690s. That trial involved the marriage of a lesser noble to a thirteen-year-old girl, a girl who was then seduced by a priest. The cuckolded husband—humiliated, jealous—murdered his young wife and her entire family. He was arrested, tried, and beheaded. The trial was not about whether or not the husband committed the crime, but whether or not, as husband, he was within his rights to kill his adulterous wife and her "accomplices."

Our project, the project Juan wished to pass to me, didn't concern any of the particulars of that trial. *Don't feel you need to keep them in your head, nene.* Juan only brought up Browning because the poet raised pertinent questions about the very act of composition. More than simply retelling the case, Browning meditates on past and present, art and fact, source material and craftsmanship. Browning compares the old yellow book he'd found to gold, and he compares himself to a goldsmith; the pure hard metal of fact made malleable by the alloy of his imagination.

This that I mixed with truth, motions of mine
That quickened, made the inertness malleable
O' the gold was not mine—what's your name for this?

*W*hat's your name for this?

From what I could gather, there were three stories Juan wanted to alloy: (1) the story of how I'd arrived at the Palace—my whore stories, he called them—told in snatches, in the dark, for his amusement; tales I found myself stretching, as I had this megalomaniacal fantasy that the stories kept him alive and in the room with me, and so I tried never to reach the final sentence; (2) the story for which he extracted the promise, the story of the *Sex Variants* study itself, Jan Gay's story, to be told after Juan's death (*But promise me, nene, you'll bend, and lie, and invent, make the inertness malleable. I promise, Juan.*); (3) the final story, Juan's own, though he'd never admit it.

III

THE KINSHIP

This enactment, at times threatening, at other times fascinating, poses a question that turns into a riddle.

—PATRICIA GHEROVICI,
The Puerto Rican Syndrome

PSYCHOPATHOLOGIC REACTION PATTERNS
IN THE ANTILLES COMMAND

MAURICIO RUBIO, *Major, MC, USAR*
MARIO URDANETA, *Captain, MSC, USAR*
JOHN L. DOYLE, *First Lieutenant, MC, USAR*

A GROUP of striking psychopathologic reaction patterns, precipitated by minor stress in persons with well-defined character disorders, has been observed in a limited section of the insular (Puerto Rican) personnel of the Antilles Command. Because of their clinical resemblance to more serious conditions such as schizophrenia and epilepsy, these behavior disorders present a problem in medical management and administrative disposition.

Another night, Juan spoke of the forced institutionaliza-
tion of our people, what he called the dark psychohistory
of American medicine. He explained how up until 1974, the
American Psychiatric Association included homosexuality in the
Diagnostic and Statistical Manual of Mental Disorders, which Juan
referred to as the biblia loca; how to be queer was unequivocally
to be insane, in need of cure; and how the 1974 removal of homosexuality from the *DSM* was so bitterly contested in the psychiatric community that six years later, in 1980, a new diagnosis,
ego-dystonic homosexuality, was created for the biblia loca's third
edition. Apparently this diagnosis was a kind of truce, an olive
branch extended to the significant portion of psychologists who
insisted on pathologizing "abnormal" sexuality.

"Here's the definition, nene—you ready?"
    "Will there be a quiz? Should I take notes?"
    "I can stop any time."
    "What, I'm not allowed to tease?"
    "You may. You may also listen."
    "Damn, Juan, all right . . ."
    "The definition is in two parts: firstly, *a persistent lack of hetero-
sexual arousal, which the patient experiences as interfering with initi-
ation or maintenance of wanted heterosexual relationships*; secondly,
*persistent distress from a sustained pattern of unwanted homosexual
arousal.* A bit of trick, no? If, say, no adult has ever spoken positively, or even neutrally about homosexuality, and yet they refer-
enced it frequently enough, in jokes, and questions, and hostile

accusations, it would be very hard for an effeminate boy of seventeen, a boy like you were, say, to desire his own desires, would it not? And technically this made you disordered, perverse. Eventually this diagnosis was thrown out as well, but the connection between abnormal sexuality and mental illness survives, and not just with Bible thumpers, but in conservative pockets of the psychiatric industry itself. Especially back then, in that place where we were locked up, on that bench—"

"Sure. I might not know the historical particulars, but I know the general outline; I lived it, with you. This all just seems a bit . . ."

"*Pedantic* is the word you're looking for."

"Don't pout."

"How long, nene, did you believe you were crazy?"

"Am I not?"

"When you took all those pills, back in that place, what did you think you were up to?"

"Did it hurt your feelings? I've always wondered that."

"It wasn't *my* feelings you were aiming to hurt. But listen. You'll forgive me for returning to the pedantic mode, but let's go back to the biblia loca for a moment. If you move along, you'll find another diagnosis, introduced in the 1950s, by army doctors, a condition with which I was first diagnosed when they brought me to the nuthouse: Puerto Rican Syndrome."

"In the *DSM*? That's not a thing."

"As I live and breathe."

"As you die and breathe."

"Wicked child."

"I don't believe it. How can you make a syndrome of a people?"

"What's that vulgar little expression you're so fond of . . ."

"It makes no sense, Juan."

"*. . . I shit you not.*"

PATTERNS OF REACTION

The most outstanding reaction pattern is characterized by a transient state of partial loss of consciousness, most frequently accompanied by convulsive movements, hyperventilation, moaning and groaning, profuse salivation, and aggressiveness to self or to others in the form of biting, scratching, or striking; and of sudden onset and termination. Less often there is complete flaccidity. The duration varies from an isolated crisis of a few minutes to a series, lasting a few hours in the convulsive form and up to two days in the flaccid variety. The reaction produced by the episode in the immediate environment appears to directly influence its duration; the greater the secondary gains, the longer it lasts. The crises are quite spectacular, and when they take place in the company area or at home they cause great alarm and confusion to those around the patient and, in some instances, immediate removal of the source of stress. They also bring considerable attention and special privileges to the patient, and when he is brought to the hospital and placed in seclusion in a cool, semidarkened room, his symptoms usually subside in a few minutes.

From Rodriguez Army Hospital, APO 851, New York, N. Y.

When Juan was a child, the world had mumbled, tinkled with awe, and he would get caught inside that awe, caught by the skimming lines of sunlight in a glass of water, and he would stare and stare, trying to understand how light had come to glint and sparkle in his little glass (*Amazing to think, nene, that light sparkles, that light dances. All for whom?*) or else he'd be captured by the smeared grease of a palm print across the windowpane, invisible from all but one angle—something small like this would get him thinking about worlds hidden and revealed. It always began with a grave need to understand, but quickly moved outside understanding, outside language. His eyes would lock and his mouth slowly open, as if he were witnessing a horrible act in very slow motion.

Two of his sisters and one brother, an aunt, too, all occasionally slipped into dramatic seizures—ataques. Nothing too unusual. They writhed on the floor, gnashed, drooled, sputtered little hums from the backs of their throats—but Juan would only stare. At some point in his young mind, he came up with a purely sensory theory about the ataques' root cause, a theory he found impossible, even as an adult, to put into words.

"Black hairs like spiders' legs above and below Papi's knuckles . . . the torque of a slap across the face . . . Mami, keening, electricity, mascara . . . a snippet of nursery rhyme on a loop: 'arroz con leche, se quiere casar' . . . all the detritus and minor shocks of corporeal difference . . . the strangeness, the tactile perversities, somehow forced inside the bony bodies of myself and my sisters and my brother and my mother . . . trapped under the skin, and no surprise when, one day, the rupture, the force and froth . . . and even now, nene, the words spilling out of my mouth are so far and so close to the essential ineffable, that I both surprise and disappoint myself."

J uan had been there, witness to the very first violent seizure of his eldest sister. He remained calm. They were, after all, wild children, especially when out of their father's eyesight, and the flailing grotesquery of the body was their specialty. Juan remembered his sister convulsing on the floor of the girls' shared bedroom, remembered the black handwoven rug confetti-speckled with bits of colored rag. He doesn't remember if he called for his folks, or how they arrived, or how it came to be that both were home at the same time, but he does remember their reaction: a calm recognition in his father's eyes, the sudden seriousness in his mother, this absolute reversal of their natural states. The lasting shock from that day was not the seizure—no surprise his sister might succumb to a contorting madness, what with all the erotic chaos, the trembling energy, the too-muchness of that home, of childhood itself—but he was surprised to find his father even capable of that kind of terrible calming care, or his mother capable of such seriousness, such focus. This was the quality of attention he had always sought from each, and now, with certainty, he knew the cost.

"Though again, all of this so far from being understood in words, but some other sensory language—the skin around my mother's eyes, the gentle bracing stance of my father, a scent even, indescribable; a change in the pheromones of parenting."

These episodic crises are spectacular and often simulate more serious psychiatric entities, particularly when the persons concerned are examined from the viewpoint of a different culture and language. When the sources of stress are removed, however, a basic overly dependent, emotionally unstable personality becomes evident. Neurotic symptoms are completely absent in the intervals between episodes. Attempts to rehabilitate patients with these character disorders are impeded by their extreme dependency needs and the secondary gains they derive from their illness.

But answer the question. About the pills, what were you up to?"

"I don't know. Killing myself?"

"Oh, come off it. You knew you'd be found."

"No, you're right, Juan. I did."

"So beneath the surface, just below your consciousness—try to remember what was going through your mind. Close your eyes. What motivated you, in the deep, in the realm of the symbolic?"

"I remember feeling very decided, very calm . . . I remember how difficult I found it, physically, swallowing pill after pill . . . I remember gagging, my throat closing, and the sounds I made, like a cat bringing up a hairball . . . I remember wishing I could somehow speed things along . . . I knelt on the floor at the side of the unmade bed and spread the pills across the mattress . . . I remember it felt like saying nighttime prayers, which my grandmother would force us to do if we went to her on an overnight visit . . . I'd always hated swallowing medicine as a kid, afraid I would choke, and the fact that I still couldn't get pills down without difficulty . . . well, it embarrassed me . . . I remember thinking that, and thinking how it was the same with the shower . . . I dreaded the shower . . . I'd avoid showering as much as I could get away with, though they watched me in that place, forced me into the stall . . . I remember thinking how this dread of the water was a holdover from childhood, when the shower had terrified me somehow . . . and these childish hang-ups lingered into my teenage years. I knew I ought to have outgrown all that, and sometimes I pretended I had, but inside, I was ruled by all these leftover morbidities."

"You say you wanted to speed things along. Maybe that's why you took all those pills, all at once?"

"How do you mean?"

"Well, what did you think the pills were for? A cure?"

"No, Juan, I don't think I ever believed that. I guess I believed they were to annihilate some dark awareness. Make it easier to live in an uncomfortable world."

"To be released of the want of the want of release."

"You're saying we're the same, you and I?"

"No, nene. I suppose I'm getting at a likeness larger than you and me."

"But you don't believe in such a thing as Puerto Rican Syndrome?"

"No, no, of course not. Though it is describing something, isn't it? And it's important to think about when these diagnoses, these studies, these pathological descriptions arise. The *Sex Variants* study, for instance, begins in New York in 1935, right at the end of what later came to be called the Pansy Craze of the late twenties and early thirties—a taste for figures like Gladys Bentley, Gene Malin, drag performances, cross-dressing, underground Harlem scenes . . . The straight culture turned its attention to our culture, and the sudden increased visibility of course provoked a backlash. If a cop walked into this room right now, with you in your little undies, lying with me, so weak, on this bed, they'd see a crime."

"What crime?"

"You are illegally cohabiting; you've snuck in, have you not? And if a journalist walked in, they'd see a story, a scandal. And if a doctor walked in, they'd see illness. And not just in my body, but in your head."

"Criminalized, stigmatized, pathologized. The student sees the lesson."

"Ha, nene, very good. Now understand that with the 1950s came a kind of Puerto Rican Craze. The advent of easy air travel changed everything about migration, especially to New York, and Puerto Ricans, increasingly visible, attracted that gaze, the cops, the journalists, the doctors. And what do you think they found? And no surprise this specific diagnosis emerges from military doctors, because other things were going on, in the army especially, with the Borinqueneers . . . and more broadly, with the long colonial relationship . . . But another lesson, as you say, for another day . . . The point is that every culture has codified ways of expressing overwhelming emotion, panic attacks, nervous breakdowns, ataques de nervios, these are all related to one another. Even in a breakdown, there are cultural codes, behaviors that render the breakdown legible, if not acceptable. You know, I'm sure, the history of the term *hysteria*?"

"I do, Juan. Basically I do. But you said the syndrome *is* describing something. What then?"

"Well, the hysterical reaction, the Hispanic panic, whatever you want to call it, to the increased Puerto Rican presence."

"White People Syndrome?"

"Colonizer Syndrome. This is being projected onto Puerto Ricans themselves, and then they are attacked. Surely that's one thing. And the other is that people living under enormous pressure do sometimes break down, don't they?"

"They do. I mean, we did."

"But then, how else would we have found each other?"

Pseudosuicidal attempts constitute the fourth clinical modality found in some of these men. Superficial scratches on the anterior aspects of the wrist, forearm, and chest, carefully inflicted with razor blades, fountain pens, or pins are the commonest means of self-injury. The ingestion of rat poison or disinfectants mixed in drinks and attempts at hanging are also frequent. All of these attempts are made in a dramatic fashion, in the presence of various people who can easily intercept the act. Many of them occur at home while on pass, and the patient makes a histrionic announcement of his intentions to his family.

My father had an explanation for the fits, the ataques, which had something to do with spirits. Tío Miguel suffered them worst, though plenty of other uncles and aunts all suffered spasms—shouting, shaking, trembling, struggling to breathe, blacking out. For Papi, ataques were common enough to warrant a wait-and-see approach; *just give the child some space*. Certainly, he did not think they'd prove debilitating, maybe even a necessary catharsis. My grandparents, you see, had been ardent practitioners of Espiritismo, and though my father considered himself more modern, more rational, and though he rejected the bulk of the folk practices, he never questioned the fact that we share the world with spirits. He never questioned the fact of the immortal soul."

"And do you? Believe in all that?"

"My mother used to say that the spirits are as lost as we are. She believed in accidental ghosts. One might show up at your door, needing assistance in crossing over, yet not knowing themselves what they needed, or how to let go, or even how to ask for help."

"You mean like how I showed up here?"

"If the shoe fits, nene. The point is neither my mother nor my father believed in possession. I don't know what did possess me, beyond what I've tried to describe, but twice in my life, this condition proved useful with white people. Once, when I was twenty or so, and the family had long since relocated from Harlem, chasing work, all the way up to Syracuse, of all places, the ataques deepened from staring spells to full-on convulsions. The seizures got me out of military service, though they landed me, instead, in an asylum—diagnosably, syndromically, Puerto Rican. So, actually, I'm not sure that counts."

"Hard no. But what about the other time?"

"I was just a small boy. I had wandered off from home, gotten myself lost. We were living in Santurce then, a great many of us in that home, and I had slipped away when no one was watching, down to the market. I realize now I couldn't have gone very far, but the intensity of the fear I felt then, the panic, short-circuited something in my brain. I stood in the street, near the flower vendor's wooden cart, staring dumbly at a little tin bucket of cut flowers. In my memory, the blossoms are birds-of-paradise, though memory deceives; they could have been anything, carnations."

"Half-real, half a bouquet of the sleeping mind?"

"Very cute."

"What happened?"

"I was found. It was Zhenya who found me. I don't remember this, but later Zhenya told me she watched as the tears had dropped, one after the other, while I stood frozen, looking and looking at the arrangement in the bucket. The world buzzed around me, the vendors hawking their wares, the women coming and going and calling out to one another in greeting. And Zhenya, who had been shopping in the market, assumed that I was so moved, so enraptured by the beauty and chaos of the world—jut as she had been as a child—that I had fallen into a form of mystical stupefaction. But then she noticed how grim, how eerie, was my stillness, zombielike, and so she came over, and squatted down beside me, and waited for me to return from wherever I had traveled in my mind. She spoke to me in an odd, foreigner's Spanish. *You are lost*, she said. *Are you?*"

Zhenya, then, was the children's book illustrator, the one responsible for the drawing of Juan tacked to the wall. After meeting Juan in the market that day, Juan served as a model for her drawings. They lived together in Viejo San Juan, Zhenya and Jan, in a colonial home split into apartments with a shared courtyard—a modest courtyard, which, at the time, seemed to Juan very grand: potted plants, a carved stone fountain, and an oversized wicker chair, where he was often hoisted up and made to sit very still while Zhenya sketched his expression.

"You were her muse?"

"If a child can be a muse to a grown woman, then yes."

"And the wicker chair? Do you remember what it looked like?"

"Enormous, with a cushioned seat. The backrest curved wide at the base and came up to a peak, like a teardrop. But nene, this chair thing, it's a strange little fetish you've got."

"And what were they like, Zhenya and Jan?"

"Aliens, really, but so familiar. You know, I was just coming on that age where tolerance for the natural effeminacy of young boys rapidly wanes. It felt to me as if the whole neighborhood had come together in a great conspiracy to correct my deportment. Close family, distant relatives, the grocer, the schoolmistress, everyone would remind me that I was a boy and should behave thusly, how to walk and speak and play, or rather how not to walk and not to speak and not to play. They said these things not in a bullying way, not out of cruelty, but as a matter of fact. Yet Zhenya and Jan, these two alien señoras, delighted in how softly I spoke, how shy I was—though they never said so outright. I don't know how I knew what I knew; some unspoken knowledge, communicated through the warmth of their indulgence."

Zhenya Gay ~~and her husband~~ *with the original "Manuelito",*

Back then, playing alone in his make-believe world, when Juan felt safe and unwatched, he had an unthinking habit of walking around on his heels, with his toes pointed up in the air, his arms straight out, and all the fingers spread on either hand. He sang to himself under his breath, soothing nonsense words.

One day he came into the kitchen to see Zhenya imitating his daydream walk, imitating his lisping child's voice, and Jan—never particularly mirthful—seated at the oak table, an audience of one, laughing and laughing, with tears in her eyes. When she spotted Juan, she swung out her arm, gesturing toward Zhenya and raising her eyebrows, as if to say, *Get a load of this! Spot-on, no?*

Juan stood frozen in the doorway, perplexed as to whether or not he was being mocked, but then Jan slapped her hand down on the tabletop, pushed back her chair, and rose; she started doing the walk, too, and though Juan was too shy to join in, he liked that, seeing them like that, together, and seeing himself, his movements, reflected in their gaiety.

They took Juan into the rainforest, where Zhenya sketched the parrots and the palms and sat down in the dirt to sketch the toads who squatted in the shade on either side of the path. Juan stood just behind Zhenya, at her shoulder, watching the image come to life, entranced. He noticed how one of the little creatures posed with particular patience, nobly, his wee chin raised, undulating, as toads do, the skin of his throat, and Juan thought he'd try harder at posing the next time he was seated in the wicker chair. He'd be still and regal, a toad prince.

A last pattern of reaction, considerably less striking than the previous four, is characterized by mild dissociation manifested by inability to concentrate, forgetfulness, loss of interest in personal appearance, some degree of preoccupation, and slight flattening of affect. It usually lasts one or two days.

J uan slept, and I found myself standing at the window, half in a dream, my hand at my neck, fingers searching absently for the cross I'd lost. This was the same cross I believed had been a gift from Juan, secreted away in the bag of personal effects, which had shown up one day after I turned eighteen and had gotten myself discharged from the nuthouse. I'd worn and worried that cross back and forth on its chain ever since, and so my fingers kept reaching for it—muscle memory. Ten years. I'd held on to it for nearly a decade. This is significant because I'm not a finder, I'm a loser. A chronic loser. A term I discovered only recently, in an essay by Anna Freud. Juan had told me where to find the essay, a dog-eared page in one of his books on psychoanalysis. I hadn't even known Freud had a daughter, and I was surprised to find the writing so clear, and accessible; surprised to find myself somewhat convinced. *Read it,* Juan said. *Know thyself.*

I read how a chronic loser constantly misplaces objects, useful or necessary—in my case, watches, keys, wallets, gloves, hats, sunglasses, eyeglasses. Sometimes they are recovered; mostly they are not. From what I understood, this is a symptom of altered libidinal processes; something misfiring in the deep, where desires are formed, making attachment difficult. (*So I'm reenacting some infantile drama of neglect? Perhaps, nene, who knows?*) But this made sense to me: In our attachments, whether to objects or others, there exists a continual fluctuation of our energies. We wish to possess, to be possessed, and to be relieved of our possessions all at once. The hoarder solves the problem of value and attachment by holding on. The chronic loser lets it all go. I routinely misplaced not only everyday items but essentials as well; I'd lost more than one passport, my birth certificate, my Social Security card, numerous licenses, an entire library's worth of books. None of these things were lost together, mind you—not all at once, as in a fire, but one by one, piecemeal. And now, in the Palace, it had come to feel as if a life itself might be misplaced.

Who knows how or when or where I lost that sketchbook, the one the nurse gave me back in that nuthouse. It came to mind when I decided to travel out here, to the desert. I thought if I found you, you might like to see the sketches inside."

"I would have, too."

"But never in all that time did I lose the necklace, the golden cross."

"Ah yes, only death may part the prisoner from his chains."

"I mean, I hadn't been careful, or clinging, or conscious of the value I'd bestowed. Wasn't until the cross went missing that I even realized I'd held on to it. I simply never took it off. Now that it's gone, now that my fingers habitually reach up to play with it, and find absence instead, I've come to feel the cross helped me to think, both to daydream and to stay rooted in the physical world, in my body. I realize, too, how ridiculous this sounds."

"A fetish object."

"You think? I've never considered myself a fetishist."

"The chairs. The imago: the gentle cop in a Stetson hat and leather boots? *Little boy, what are you doing here?* And now, as it turns out, you've got a thing for golden crosses, or perhaps for chains."

"Oof, Juan. I'm a cliché, aren't I?"

"But an amusing one, nene. Go on. Close your eyes. Take me through the associations."

My father was a man who both did and did not wear chains. When I was around nine or ten years old, he went undercover, moved from being a regular state trooper to a narc. This involved him accentuating his "roots," by which I mean it was necessary and expected of him to perform a kind of ghetto authenticity; to speak Spanish and Spanglish and jive with the older generations and a less poetic, more vulgar contemporary slang with the young ones; to embody the intimidation and charm of a gangster. His work car, which my brothers and I loved to sneak inside, had tinted windows and was pimped, as we said at the time. My father was not an actual gangster. In his home life, and in our white working-class town, he was aspirational, busy elevating his station, keeping up with the neighbors. He left the house and returned dressed like all the other dads. We rarely saw him in his work costume. Only on the rarest of occasions, for reasons unknown to us, would he break out the flash: the diamond stud earring, the gold chains, the gold cross, the medallions, the gold watch. (When alone in the house, I used to hunt for this jewelry, unsuccessfully. Eventually, I gave up, assuming it must all be kept in the lockbox under the bed, next to his gun.) He'd sag his jeans, and we'd imitate his strut. "Put some stank on it," he'd say, and we'd try and mostly fail. The persona that floated up to the surface in those moments was uncanny, this other, gangster father, drawn from both stereotype and some mysterious essence he kept hidden from us. Upstate, I was used to everyone projecting cool onto my father, no matter how corny he might act, due simply to his Brooklyn accent and brown skin, but

in those moments of transformation—in the flash of the flash—
an actual, almost tangible coolness radiated, emanated from
inside.

My father was a proud man, and moody. He could be sentimental, loving, hilarious, but he could also explode into violence. My mother explained this had to do with the prejudice and indignities of poverty he'd dealt with in childhood. Explaining away the "bad father" and redirecting us toward the "good enough father" is so often one of a mother's covert responsibilities. Yet whatever or whomever flashed in those moments, when he wore the charms and called forth this other persona, with both self-mockery and reverence, this trickster figure, hard and cool—well, I did not want this man explained away. I wanted him to stay. And to my child mind it seemed the charm of the shadow father had everything to do with all that bling, with the charms themselves, the most mystical and magical of all, which I was not allowed to wear, or touch, being the crucifix.

"But something happened, eh niño? Something terrible, or mundane, but powerful enough to alter your relationship to this form of ostentatious, hardened masculinity?"

"Do you like the story?"

"Go on. Give me the memory. Present tense."

We drive down from our home in the boondocks six hours south, making the pilgrimage to the three-bedroom Brooklyn apartment where my aunt and uncle and abuela and five cousins all live. Other tíos and cousins are there when we arrive, and more shuffle in behind us. It's crowded, loud, the air thick—people still smoked indoors back then. I'm forced through hellos, reintroductions, prods to speak up; I'm shy. On the living room floor, the younger cousins press up close to the television, watching cartoons, which they turn louder and louder to battle the noise. Commercials play for toys and sugar cereals. I want to join the little ones, though I'm too old to do so unselfconsciously, so I inch closer and closer, when in walks a young man I've never seen before. He's beautiful. Apart from the uncles I know, in Brooklyn there are always new men, second cousins, half-siblings of half-siblings, somebody's boyfriend, who are introduced as "uncle" so-and-so. I don't remember this uncle's name or relation, only that I never saw him before, and I never saw him again after that day. He is beautiful. The soft luster of his skin is only accentuated by his rather severe nose and brow. Everything is crisp: his fade, the lines shaved into his eyebrows; jewelry glints all around him: a diamond stud earring, chains, a gold watch worn loose. So beautiful that the men are unafraid to acknowledge the fact, as they do now, whistling through their teeth and naming him *pretty boy*. He is probably only a teenager, but he very coolly makes the rounds of handshakes, daps, and benedictions. I stare, nakedly, as he unzips and removes his jacket. Underneath is a T-shirt printed with a cartoon rabbit, whom I recognize as the mascot of the kids' cereal Trix.

Silly Faggot, the shirt reads. *Dix are for chix.*

I don't remember any other person's reaction, though it's safe to assume some laugh and some chastise. This is the very early nineties. What do I know then? I know that the hatred of faggots has to do with AIDS, and again, in the unformed depths, I know that the hatred of faggots has also to do with me; I know it is time for me to leave the world of cartoons and sugar cereals, and I am embarrassed by the fact that I am not ready, that I keep looking backward. I know that it feels dangerous to look at this uncle, but still, I want to. I force my gaze into the middle space, below his eyes and above his message, where a crucifix hangs—and it's an exact replica of the one my father keeps hidden away somewhere in the house. That's the point of fixation, where the memory short-circuits, overloaded by the sudden double awareness of something burning in me, and a new depth to the ugliness burning out there, in the world.

OVER

o you know why we fetishize, nene? To survive our own ambivalence. Perhaps the chains, and especially the crucifix, became totems, able to absorb both hatred and desire. Perhaps in their glimmer and weight you saw a reflection of all that you wanted, and all that you feared."

"I don't know, Juan. I certainly didn't think any of that at the time. My parents divorced, and I lost my father, a gradual process that was pretty complete by the time I met you. I never really saw him again after I got out of the hospital, and I was doing everything I could to shake my mother."

"That Wildean quip comes to mind: *To lose one parent may be regarded as misfortune; to lose both looks like carelessness.*"

"That's right. I was careless with my life and their care for me, and things came to a head in a dramatic rupture, until finally I left for the city, where I was very much alone, and very broke, and then one day I was mugged."

"Oh, good. A bit of action at last."

I'm walking down some Chelsea block with a friend, leaving a club called Tunnel. This would have been September 1998, coming on five in the morning and still very dark. The kid has a knife. A few others mill around outside the club, though no one intervenes. The kid has a knife, but he's shorter and probably younger than my friend and me. We must have looked like easy marks, vulnerable, newbies to the city, eighteen and piss drunk. We laugh, partly out of a kind of nervous terror, but also because we have nothing to offer up. I turn my pockets inside out; my friend opens her purse and pulls out various objects, a lipstick, a wad of tissue, and just keeps repeating, *Look, I have nothing. We have nothing.* Neither of us has credit cards, or even wallets or phones. (No one carried phones in those days, at least no one like us.) Even our IDs are fake; we've left our real ones at home. We had just enough cash for the cover charge and spent the night downing the dregs of others' abandoned drinks. The club kids ignored us; they were all so sophisticated in their debauchery; we were bumpkins. *Bumpkins but not for long!* we had vowed, yelling into the night, stumbling down the sidewalk, into the tip of the knife. I don't remember the mugger's reaction; I don't remember how we got out of it. The memory ends with the image of my friend squatting, crapulous, and dumping her purse on the sidewalk. *I have nothing. We have nothing,* she says. And it's true.

A couple of days later, I found the gold chain with the gold cross, in the bag of my belongings, in a kind of reverse mugging, a gifting. I thought of Juan, of that place, imagined him somehow slipping the cross into my bag, but pushed away the memories; the entire experience was too fresh, and I couldn't afford to look at it directly—I needed to forget. I felt the vagaries of ownership then, the churning city, how I might be made or unmade, possessed and dispossessed at will, but never entirely alone, and I suppose I decided not to invest much in stability, ownership, not to try to hold on. And rather than exhausted, I felt exhilarated at this thought. I was so young. Scrawny. My uniform consisted entirely of printed secondhand T-shirts from the boys' section, usually with messages about Little League or summer camp or, ironically, D.A.R.E., and I began to wear them inside out, which I believed made me look more mature, and better displayed my gold necklace. I never took off the cross, not to shower, and certainly not when—as finally, finally, began to happen—men picked me up in bars and brought me home for sex.

I saw, under the sun, that the race is not to the swift . . . neither yet bread to the wise, nor yet riches to men of understanding . . . but time and chance happeneth to them all . . . Something like that."

"Jesus?"

"Old Testament. Ecclesiastes . . . though I'm a bit foggy at the moment. I can't quite recall who's speaking, nor can I recall the passage in full, the proper order of the images . . ."

"All this Bible. All this poetry. I do wish I could steal from inside your mind."

". . . but the dead know not any thing, neither have they any more a reward; for the memory of them is forgotten. Oh, bother. That's wrong. You know, nene, I think I may close my eyes now, drift off somewhere else for a bit. Tomorrow, you'll tell me about one of these men you met in the bars."

"No, no. Tomorrow is your turn. I haven't forgotten that much."

"Is it?"

"A proper story. You promised."

"A proper story, then. For an improper child."

Among the stacks of Juan's books I separated out the children's literature, all illustrated by Zhenya. Many of the books she wrote herself; others were cowritten, some with Jan. I found a couple of titles for adults as well, reissues of classics, for which Zhenya contributed images—including a very dreary illustrated edition of Oscar Wilde's *The Ballad of Reading Gaol.* Dreary in a good way. I asked Juan if he'd collected every last one of her books.

"Hunted, darling, scavenged. Anyway, the story I'm thinking of, the one I want you to find, is one of her later publications, from 1965, a book she wrote herself. African savanna animals, all gathered around a watering hole, when suddenly appears a strange new creature, a young boy. As you read, I want you to imagine an underground queer bar, pre-Stonewall. Think of it all as extended metaphor. The book is titled *Who's Afraid?*"

"*Who's Afraid?*"

"Not I."

"Funny, Juan.

"*Not I, Not I, said the spider to the fly.*"

"That's not how it goes."

"How goes it?"

"*I, said the fly, with my little eye, I watched him die.*"

The local watering hole. Maybe it's midday. A quiet, un-happy hour. At any rate, it's only regulars. When Elephant remarks he's so hungry, he's afraid he'll eat all the grass, Lion teases him. Lion is afraid of nothing. Elephant claims it's just a figure of speech, but then Leopard pounces and teases Lion in return, insinuating that Lion's bravado is more posture than substance, and everyone's afraid of something. It goes on like this: sniping, camp, confusion, escalation. A fuss. Badger feels he is forever missing out, so low is he to the ground. Monkey laments, *All fuss, no feathers.* Which sets Hyena off, his infectious laughter dissipating the tension.

Really! mumbles Hippopotamus and lowers his head under the water."

"Everyone is nursing something. Lion his meat, Leopard his bone, Monkey his banana. All the animals are male. Giraffe, one imagines, is the barkeep, stretching for his tips, his tender green leaves. When things get too testy, it's Giraffe who tries to keep the peace. Lion and Leopard are hustlers, machos, though only Lion is king, and Leopard can barely contain his envy. Elephant is high-strung, middle-class. Badger is insecure about his body and his status. Monkey and Hyena are sissy queens; they know how and when to laugh. Hippopotamus is a drunk.

This watering hole, like all watering holes of its kind, nene, is subject to a police raid at any moment, or a mafioso popping in for his collection, or a lost tourist from the straight world. Occa-sionally, men come in just to harass. Anyone unknown could be undercover, vice. At the sound of a new arrival, they all drop into masculine poses, or burrow down into themselves. Badger curls himself into a ball.

Only it's a new boy. Wanting. Terrified. Giraffe says gently, *Don't be afraid. Please come out and let us look at you.*

Elephant begs, *Please come out, do.*"

"You see, nene, the way I understand it, historians locate a lexico-logical shift in the meaning of *coming out* to the midsixties. After Stonewall, the sense of coming out will be firmly attached to *the closet*, a place of skeletons, isolation, claustrophobia. But no meta-phor of the closet existed in the decades prior. The original sense of the term *coming out* was borrowed from debutante cultures, as much a fixture of Black elite society as Southern white, where one came out into the expectant world. One announced one's arrival, perhaps literally, at a ball. The drags. Or one wandered down into the local fag watering hole. Either way, one entered. One arrived."

"Do you think it's possible Zhenya wrote the book for you, Juan? For the child you were? Or the young man she knew you'd become?"

"You like the story?"

"It's all there, isn't it? Go on, do the rest."

"From each according to his ability, to each according to his needs. Monkey fetches bananas for the boy's hunger. Elephant mounts the boy onto his own back. They ask again and again what else he might need, how else they might allay his fears, but the boy doesn't quite know how to put words to the feeling of defamil-iarization, nor his discomfort, which is existential. *You're all nice, but I'm still a little bit afraid—it's very far from the ground up here.* Hyena distracts the boy with humor, teaches the boy to laugh, queerly, down into the abyss.

In procession, they escort the boy back to where he belongs.

I, announces Monkey, *will ride on the elephant's back with plenty of bananas for the boy.* Winks and smirks.

We'll bring up the rear, say Lion and Leopard.

And I'll bring up the rear of the rear. Whooo-ooooop! Hyena mocks how easy it might be to flip these two supposed studs.

On the way, Hippopotamus, drunk, slips on a banana peel. Much laughter at his expense, which Hippopotamus does not appreciate. He decides to head back to the watering hole. He needs a drink. *The water will soothe me.*

The rest arrive on a troubling, sprawling scene. The boy explains it's his mother and father and brothers and sisters and aunts and uncles and all his friends. *It's everyone!*

Dear me, are you sure? asks Elephant. The animals and the boy keep just out of sight, eavesdropping. The family believes the boy to be stolen. Not wayward, not lost.

They're saying they'll find and punish whoever it was. A shiver runs through the group. They know this routine. They whisper and worry. The boy, in his naivete, insists there is no problem. *You're my friends and I want you to meet my mother and father and*—But the animals cut him off. They are starting to freak. They whisper among themselves; they need to get gone, fast.

Small boy, do you mind if we don't meet your family today? I'm really worried about Hippopotamus, and I think we should go back, says Elephant. The boy understands now. He needs to go the rest of the way, straight ahead, by himself. Still, how will the animals know he arrived safely?

Why, I'll laugh like you, Hyena, says the boy.

Of course. And we leave the story here, the boy back with his family, and the animals eager to get back to the relative safety of the watering hole, but waiting, anxiously, for the sign from the boy. And then they hear it, unmistakable, the mark of the pansy, fearless; that high and happy bark; that scavenger's yelp. That queer cry of recognition, the unmistakable laugh of the hyena."

IV

THE PALACE
AT 4 A.M.

Out of Adamant Co-op
men in "overhauls" step into evening rising
in long-shadowed bluish haze to gold and pink
by Sodom Lake (was it that any Bible name
was an OK name?) and boys stare unabashed
and unaggressive not what the man on the bus fled
from his one day job talking excitedly about
"teen-age Puerto Rican tail-bait" and
"You can *have* New York!" . . .
—**JAMES SCHUYLER,** "Now and then"

And then I felt, or sensed, from the purple black of the soundless sky, that we were in the nethermost opposition of the night, when it's hard to believe the day will ever break.

Psst. Nene. You asleep?"

"Never, Juan."

"Well, keep your eyes closed."

"They're open, Juan. I was wondering about the time. It's so dark and quiet. Dawn comes later and later, don't you think? I could get up and open the curtains wide, if you like. I'll bet it's three or four in the morning. We might see the stars."

"*In the Palace at 4 a.m.* What's that from?"

"No idea."

"Leave the curtains. Close your eyes. Give me one of your whore stories, only make it a film."

"A film?"

"You've read Puig?"

"No. I don't think so. But Liam and I used to tell each other the plots of films, in the night. I must have mentioned that, eh, Juan?"

"Stop saying my name like that."

"Like what?"

"*In the Palace at 4 a.m. you walk from one room to the next by going through the walls.* What's that from?"

"I'd like to see the other rooms."

"You really ought to know your fairy forefathers. Puig and Piñero and the rest. The plays, especially. What will you do when you bump into these eminent maricones in hell? How embarrassed you'll be not to know."

"I don't suppose Albee counts, or Tennessee Williams? *Flores para los muertos?*"

"They carved a place where there was no place. But tell me a film. Eyes closed. Pause a moment, to compose."

"Okay, Juan . . . You know, come to think of it, I have read some Piñero. Though perhaps not enough to recognize him in hell . . ."

"And for God's sake, nene, take your time."

A fog-lined street. A streetlamp. A young man, and an older, slightly taller, bearded man, with thin red veins bolting across his nose. They huddle together in a halo of light, midconversation. The man seems to be feeling the kid out a bit, or vice versa, but finally the situation clarifies: the older man offers the kid money, seventy dollars, to pose in diapers.

Cut to an ancient four-story Victorian house; the man lives in the attic, in the old maids' quarters. The kid follows the man up a winding back staircase, up and up, the steps creaking and their boots clopping and the noise reverberating against the walls. They sound like a stampede, like a reckoning force.

The bearded man has many keys for his many locks, and when the door finally swings open, the kid staggers inside and flops onto the bed.

"Bring me a glass of water, would you?" he asks.

"What's his name, the kid?"

"Let's call him Sal. Short for Salvatore."

"He's a drunk?"

"Shh, Juan, just listen. But yes, a little."

The kid spreads himself across the mattress, spreads his arms and legs and takes up all the space. After a while, the bearded man comes and offers him a short tumbler filled to the brim. Sal must sit up and take the glass delicately into both hands, stretching his neck to sip without tilting. The man watches a long moment, then sits on the edge, timid-like, and unlaces his shoes.

"You're a nice kid, aren't you?" the man says, suddenly turning to look Sal in the face.

Sal asks the man to save him, but he doesn't say it out loud. He says it with his eyes, with shy looks.

The diaper is an adult diaper, designed for the elderly, but obviously the idea is for Sal to look and act like a baby—he never puts it on. He undresses slowly, then undresses the bearded man even more slowly, then rolls him onto his stomach and gets up on top. There's no score to this movie, not yet, only the normal sounds: the movement of the two of them on the bed, and some shouting from outside, which floats in through the open window. The man huffs and puffs, and Sal jams his fingers into the man's curls. Their bodies are real, not movie-star bodies; the man is white, a little pasty, speckled here and there, and the kid has no real definition, though he's thin and young, and the sex is real, too, the entrance isn't easy, the man has to stop and tell the boy to use more spit; all a little clumsy, but not unsexy. Soon the man is cursing and they're finishing, and we cut to the title card:

STARVE A RAT

That's when the score begins. Classical music. Soft and lovely. And we cut to flashback: Sal is sitting with some girls, in the moonlight, by the side of a river, and they're all laughing, or rather, one girl is causing the rest to laugh; she's growling at Sal, like a dog. Zoom in on her dark-painted lips, pulled back, baring her shiny teeth, the pink of her mouth inside. That's it. Cut back to the attic room, though the music continues.

"What is the music?"

"I don't really know classical music. You tell me."

"Satie."

"Okay, then."

"But really, nene, a flashback at the moment of climax?"

[163]

"What, too cheesy? They're important. These girls."

"I should think so. Arriving as they do."

"You're right, I should leave them out of this."

"No, no. Now they're here, they're very welcome. Go on."

The bearded man returns to the bed from the record player—it's his music they're listening to, Satie. Sal lies on his back and the man winces as he climbs into bed and lies down beside. They stare up at the ceiling, which peaks in the middle and slopes down to the floor.

"You remember the first time you ever bit into a piece of corn on the cob?" Sal asks him. "You remember how it seemed? Like everything all at once? The sweet of the corn juice, the warm butter, the skin of it between your teeth? Remember? Man, the first time I tasted corn on the cob, I spit it out, I spit it all over the table."

The bearded man laughs silently, blowing air through his nose. "I'd like to be surprised," Sal says. "You like surprises?"

The man says nothing. Both are quiet for a long time: their breath slows and deepens, their heart and lungs inside their chests, doing their steady work, blood and air. Sal matches his breath exactly to the man's, finds his rhythm. The record ends. Zoom in on Sal as he drifts into sleep; voices and noises rise up from the street, echo in Sal's mind, and the face of the snarling girl starts to resurface, the river; the images and sounds arrange themselves into the beginnings of a dream . . .

"You can't sleep here," the man says, and Sal's eyes snap open.

"Says who?"

"How old are you, kid, really? You're not nineteen."

The kid is nineteen years old.

"I'm a newborn," he says, laying it on thick. "I ain't even born."

The bearded man laughs his silent laugh.

"Why don't you tell me the truth. Tell me a true story," he says, and Sal looks as if he could kiss him. "Tell me something about your father," he suggests. "Make it terrible." And Sal looks as if he could punch his face with kisses.

Still, he tells a story about a beach his father and he had once walked together, all the way to the end, where they found a silent emptiness.

"Another flashback? I hope they don't spend the whole film chatting in bed. We get quite enough of that around here."

"Okay, fine. They'll get up soon."

"Atta boy."

"But, Juan? I'm never going back, am I? I mean . . . there's no leaving . . . this . . ."

"Shh. The movie's starting."

We flash back: a beach scene. First the crowds, the blankets and the boom boxes and the perspiring, sand-crusted bottles of beer, the mango hawkers, the orange-clad lifeguards—and then, way off in the distance, the boy and his father. The camera takes its time catching up, until we close in, a tight shot on the two of them. The sun is slacking off, and the wind is picking up. The father says they could imagine themselves anywhere, on any shore in any country, or on an island not yet discovered. The boy is barefoot and bare-chested, and cold, wearing thin hand-me-down swim trunks. The father wears something short and flashy, powder blue, with snap pockets and a Velcro fly.

The boy is asking the father questions about the time before the boy was born, and the father asks him to consider how young he was, just a punk, when he became a father. More of these kinds of questions; more of these kinds of answers. A lot of the conversation is carried away in the wind, or drowned out by the breaking waves.

They come upon a sun-bleached plastic Hula-Hoop and the boy drags it behind him through the sand. They walk and walk until they reach the remains of a campfire. The boy digs through the ashes and finds a few burnt-out aluminum cans and bottle caps. He pulls his charcoal-black fingers across his body, paints himself in zebra stripes, and the father curls his fingers into the square shape of a camera.

"You know any tricks?" the father asks, nodding his chin at the Hula-Hoop.

"I can spin it on my neck," the boy says.

"Let me get a picture of that."

Cut back to bed. To the bearded man, Sal says, "Try to see my paps: a patch of black curls in the center of his chest, big nipples like soft cones, and those shorts, with snap pockets. Try to see how strong he was. Now picture a water fountain on this beach—one of those cement pillars with stones and bits of shells pressed into all the sides. And picture me. All along I'm thinking we're walking toward that water fountain, Paps and me, but then at that moment I remember that this water fountain I'm thinking of, it ain't on the beach at all, but on a park path through the woods! I don't think I ever was so thirsty."

"Thirsty," repeats the bearded man. He sounds satisfied—and Sal knows what he's doing to him, the way he conjures the story.

Cut to the beach. The Hula-Hoop is coated in a thin layer of sand and scratches the boy's neck as he whips it around, but he's a natural. Paps takes a long while composing his shot, crouching, then rising up on his toes, then coming in close, then to this side, then the other. All the while, the hoop swings round his neck.

Sal says to the bearded man: "See Paps? He's giggling. I never seen him giggle. And he keeps telling me I look wild. Wild, he says, over and over, just wild. So I don't stop. But the thing is, I'm strangling myself, and as the hoop goes round I'm getting dizzier and dizzier, but he loves it."

Cut back to the bed; Sal turns on his side to look at the man. "Wild, he says, and I'm thirsty and angry and scared, but he's taking shots of me, and he's giggling, so I go on, strangling myself." The man turns in the bed, mirroring Sal's pose; he looks at the kid, square.

[166]

"For him?"

"For him."

"You are a nice kid, aren't you?"

Save me, Sal says. He's asking to be saved.

They fall asleep. End scene.

"Would you really talk like that? To your lovers? All *Gee willikers, mister, I ain't had nothing but possum to eat for days.*"

"I did, Juan. Sometimes I did."

"And it worked?"

"Only when I half believed it myself . . . which was embarrassingly easy to do."

"Go on, nene. I like the film."

In the morning, they're still in bed. The bearded man offers Sal his hand to shake and tells him his name for the first time: Norwood; he explains that he was named after the village of his father. Sal tells him that would make him Brooklyn, or more specifically, Gowanus. And so that's the name he calls Sal, from that morning on until the end of the film, he calls him Gowanus, and sometimes Little Go-Go, and sometimes simply G.

Norwood's sloping attic walls are striped with wooden beams of very old, very serious wood, and though the kid can only see their rusted, flat heads, Norwood explains that the nails inside are square instead of round, and that they were each handmade by a blacksmith.

"I don't love old things," he tells Norwood, who blinks at him. "I'm not that kind of person."

Norwood hands the kid his clothes and plods off to shower. Sal dresses, then straightens the sheets on the bed and folds back the comforter. The kitchen is cramped, dishes in the sink, a tiny square of four-paned window. The kid literally rolls up his sleeves and gets to work. Ingratiating. He keeps turning around to watch how Nor-

wood moves through his morning. There he is, wet-haired and tow-
eled, opening the plastic lid of a record player and putting on an
album—a woman with an unlovely voice, who tries earnestly and
without embarrassment to make herself sound lovely. Sal opens the
cabinets, finds and puts on coffee. There's Norwood, looking pon-
derously at the large, unused diaper and placing it into the bottom
drawer of a bureau.

Not wild, not diapered; the kid wants to be lovely.

There are mugs of different sizes and colors, and he picks one for
Norwood and one for himself. The way he picks the mug is more than
short-term. Then Sal, at the stove, frying eggs, starts talking about
how he's traveling light. At the moment, all he owns is a canvas duffel
bag's worth of clothing. The bag is so overstuffed, he's had to take two
lockers at the bus station and split the clothes between.

"I'm hoping to land," he says, but when he turns around Norwood
is in the other room; he's heard nothing.

"How old are you?" Sal calls out to him.

There's some gray in the man's beard, and the veined nose, the
paunch, the soft hairs inside his ears, but the skin of his thighs and ass
is taut and muscled underneath. Record players and folk singers are
only barely obsolete, so it's hard to know what angle he's taking with
all that.

Norwood comes into the kitchen, dressed now for his day. He looks
at the steaming eggs.

"After this," he says, "I'd better walk you on down."

Norwood's not bitter—but the kid, he must fight hard, all the time,
not to be. Sal asks him if he remembers the story he told last night.
Norwood's fingers form around an air-camera, which he brings to his
face, pressing on the air-button and saying, "Snap."

"Don't!" The kid slams his fist on the counter, losing that particular
fight.

"Don't what?"

"Don't take my picture. Don't be my father. Don't walk me on
down."

Cut to Sal and the girls, by the river, though all very serious now. They stare into the water while in voice-over we hear:

"My friends and I used to play a game called Two Truths and a Lie—but the trick was just to tell three lies, or three true things; the trick was to let no one ever really figure you out: Take my picture. Be my father. Let me stay right here.

A very white town, and all the girls were white girls, and very tough. Those nights we shared a bottle of something pilfered and did not look at each other; we looked at the river, and the truths and lies were not kind, but terrible. At times, after one of us had finished speaking, there would be a silence so deep and hurt that the only sound was the suck of our lips pulling smoke in through our filters and pushing it back out into the night. We had to say what we had to say, stories about how lost and hopeless and mean we felt, and you could trace every story back to our families, and if you poked around a little in those families you'd find our fathers, men gone half-crazy with the spirit, or the spirits, or made mean from shit work and a broken body, and sex. And we looked at the river, little goosies sitting side by side, and we knew the river would never dry up—all of this was very recent, very close to me, all the time."

"You mean to say that—to the flashbacks—we're now adding voice-over?"

"Fine. Maybe none of that is necessary. Maybe the kid just stands there in the kitchen, in a trance, blacking out."

Cut to Norwood placing a hand on Sal's shoulder. Sal jerks.
"Sit," says Norwood. "Look. You've made coffee."
The kid folds his arms and sticks out his lip in a mime of petulance.
"And anyway, G, I wanted to ask you, last night, that story, what

were the questions you were asking him, your father, I wanted to know that."

The kid swings back into good humor.

"You liked that story?" He tries to look bashful. "You really want to know?"

The coffee tastes bitter. He takes Norwood's cup and sloshes it into the sink before he can even get a sip. End scene.

"A brat."

"Sure, Juan. But at that time in life, as far as I could make out, there was one way to get a person to fall in love with you—thrashing."

"*Thrashing?* Well, there's a fine word . . . Somewhere between the utility of *threshing* and the waste, the violence, of *trashing*. That's the secret, is it? Had I only known . . ."

"In and out of bed, all the time, thrashing."

A montage now. The kid continues to make money in this way, which Norwood teases about being the oldest way on earth. The deal he strikes with Norwood is that every few weeks he'll go down to the clinic, but he does not go down to the clinic. The fact is the kid is capable of telling very big lies.

We see him meet a variety of men, with a variety of fetishes, but they themselves all fall within a narrow range, a type. And he's the type of nineteen-year-old they employ—which is to say thin and baby-faced in the physical sense, and aged and angry (but not yet completely embittered) in the emotional sense, which is to say he knows how to look at them with bunny-rabbit vulnerability sometimes, the before and after times, and with contempt and disgust other times, business times. The men are all white, every last one of them. The kid's ethnicity is ambiguous, muddled. They ask, Are you part Egyptian? Yes! Dominican? Yes! *Then the kid lowers his eyebrows and asks them,* But how did you know? *In this way, he finds out a lot about geography and geopolitics—these men, they are proud to be such excellent guessers and love to tell him about the countries he's from.*

But types, types; everyone knows the drill. They're playing a game they'll never tire of playing, like naughty, inexhaustible children, and the kid, he prances and poses and beats them up, and he wants, needs, to be lovely.

Only Norwood knows his true origins: the small town, that river, his tough girls. Another flashback then: he's telling Norwood about the spot where they would sit, a cement slab guarding an enormous drainage pipe. We see all the rainwater slushing down the gutters, directed to this pipe, and then we see the group of them climb up on the cement slab to watch the water flow out into the river. They share a joint. Sal is having trouble with the tough white boys in the hallways and on the paths and inside the town's one diner. He's an easy target for the kind of ammunition boys like that keep stockpiled. And his friends, they understand all that, but they've known these boys since childhood, and they don't want to give them up, and so they expect him to laugh it off; they demonstrate to Sal how to laugh it off, how to roll his eyes and flip the bird and spit—we sense none of those options are really available to him. None of those boys was going to jump a girl in public, but boys like him are jumped and re-jumped and humiliated. He starts to say something along those lines, but stops himself, tucks his head down. He loves these girls, and he wants to show it. I mean, he's clearly a fag, anyone watching can see that, but still, one of the girls leads him to the woods just beyond the drainage pipe, for lessons. He pushes his tongue into her mouth, fumbles his fingers in her panties, and she tries to show him what to do next, but he pulls away, tells her he's too stoned to get it up.

—————

"And what happens to them all, nene? Do they ever get out? Leave that town?"

Cut to Sal and Norwood sitting in a bar. The kid finishes the story, saying that what he really wanted was for those girls to protect him and he could not always trust them to do so—and sometimes maybe he hated them for that.

We recognize the bar as the same one where the kid picks up a lot of his employers. The place is on a corner lot and shaped like a triangle. Two of the walls are all glass and the third wall is the bar itself, so folks mostly sat with their backs to the bartender and their elbows propped up behind them, watching life pass by on the street. A number of bars concentrate in that neighborhood, all of them louder and younger and more crowded, and so a lot of men pass by the window wearing the kinds of clothes one wears to loud, young, crowded places—denim jeans snug in the crotch and oversized, glinting belt buckles. The clientele of this corner bar is older, some very old; no one ever dances, and for this, and another, meaner reason, the bar is nicknamed the Glass Coffin.

Inside, lovely, earnest music plays very soft and low. It's nearly closing time; a quiet night even for a place like this. Instead of dancing, the few men left remain seated, and now and then one or the other raises his arm in recognition of a tune he particularly enjoys and then kind of floats his hand through the air and mouths the words. Passing by, you might think they're casting spells. Sitting backward at the bar is awkward, and the elderly fellow next to Sal just cannot manage, so he faces forward and keeps his eyes on the angled mirror, which captures the street, all those flashy dressers flowing by the windows, endlessly.

"What happened to them?" Norwood asks. "Did any of them ever get out? Leave that town?"

"Very cute, nene. I don't mind being teased. But this feels like the end. You've rushed through. We need to see more of what the relationship was like between the two."

"You mean Norwood and the kid?"

"That's right."

"Well, yeah, I guess I skipped the middle of the film. You see them kiss a lot, on the lips; you see Norwood ask the kid to use less tongue. Some nights Norwood shyly nods his head in the direction of the bureau where he keeps that ridiculous diaper and asks if they might try again, but the kid holds Norwood's face and directs it back to his and shuts him up with kisses. Norwood designs jewelry. We get the impression that Norwood earns more than enough money to move somewhere larger. He leaves the apartment each morning and goes to his office, or studio, or wherever one goes to design jewelry."

"Some shots of him at work would be nice."

"Yes, tiny hammers and pliers and one of those magnifying monocles that attaches to a headlamp. Shots like that. Each morning, Norwood walks the kid on down; he's not allowed to stay. Norwood encourages him to come back to him late, past supper. Most nights he pours them gin and tonics and they talk. Sal tells him, again and again, about his town and his crew of tough girls, and his paps. The kid's duffel bag is in a corner by the bed and his clothes spill out and pile around, and sometimes he returns to find them all stuffed back inside, the dirty mixed with the clean, and the bag sealed up by its drawstring. Sal has this vision that one night he will come back and find the clothes washed and folded and placed into drawers. In bed, he allows Norwood to call him his son, his little baby boy."

"Go on, nene, with your bar scene."

Interior: The Glass Coffin. Norwood and Sal at the bar.

"Left town? Where would they go?" The kid thrashes, allows his voice to rise. "Here? Here?"

The elderly fellow sitting next to the kid at the bar elbows Sal gently. Sal looks at the elbow, then down the sleeve of his cashmere sweater to the blue-veined hand wrapped around his glass, a gold ring on the pinky, then up at the elderly fellow's face.

"Is this man bothering you?" he asks, indicating Norwood.

"Maybe." Sal laughs. Gumption, his paps would have called it. "You know what? Buy me a drink, and I'll let you bother me, too."

"Hmph," says this fellow. He appreciates Sal with his eyes; the kid isn't worth much. Not gumption; presumption. The fellow turns his attention to the bartender. "I don't know why you allow these children in off the street; this one can't be of age."

"He's all right," says the bartender.

"It depresses me."

"He's all right," repeats the bartender.

"Oh, I forgot, but in the earlier montage, you see the bartender follow the kid into the bathroom and push him against a wall, thumb around in his underwear a bit, while the kid stares silently forward and clenches."

"He doesn't like it?"

"Oh, he probably does. But from the outside, you can't tell one way or the other."

"One of those cinematic bartenders in suspenders? Dish towel hanging over the shoulder?"

"Sure, but, like, you never once see him dry a glass."

Back in the bar, Norwood blushes and leans across.

"Be nice," he says to the man, and Sal laughs gauchely, head thrown

back, which deepens Norwood's blush. Then Sal growls at the elderly fellow, and we cut back to a shot of his girl, those lips thickly painted purple-brown, and then we pull out, and there she is, a gorgeously tough girl in a little boy's used jersey from the Salvation Army, with her long, center-parted hair and her bangs, which poke into her eyes. We cut back to the bar.

"In that town, at that time," the kid says to Norwood, "almost every other pubescent girl and grown woman shaped and sculpted and tweezed away their eyebrows, but my girls all had these caterpillars hiding out beneath their bangs, and I thrilled at the sight of them."

"Caterpillars," Norwood says. Drunk.

The kid slumps. "I'm bored. Let's go."

"You don't want to finish telling me about the hometown gang?" Norwood says, teasing.

We sense that Sal could never finish. We feel these girls, real bona fide small-town girls, don't deserve to be dragged into a place like this and judged. The bar has pretty much cleared, we can sense Sal's building resentment, that he is beginning to feel like the entertainment. We'd like to see him get down from that barstool, walk out the door.

But what does he do? He starts in on the girls' mothers; he jives.

He talks about the way their mothers always kind of laughed at him, and the way some looked at him with this knowing smirk. How he was drawn to that smirk. They knew a queer, all right, but still they made sure he was fed whenever he was at the house, pushed a plate of noodles coated in butter and powdered cheese, or something microwaved, into his hands, just like they would have for any other of their daughters' boyfriends, and that was important to him.

And then it's a monologue. Sal gently spins himself in circles on the stool as he speaks.

"Our town was filled with single mothers—tough women, all of a certain type. And me and my girls, we were just like all the other townie kids in that we knew, practically to a cent, how much money *our mothers had in their purses, and how much they kept in a kitchen drawer, or a shoebox in the back of the closet; we knew whether the electric had been paid or needed to be paid; we knew the cost of every grocery that had come into the house, especially the luxury, off-limit items, the Dove bars or boxed chocolate donuts, the bubble bath, the creams and lotions. We knew what was spent on cigarettes, beer, wine, lotto. We knew how the money had been earned, up at the brewery, or waitressing, or shift work, or caring for disabled children, or cleaning. Our mothers came home from those jobs and plucked out their eyebrows into a line, filed and painted their nails and gilded their earlobes and necklines and fingers and wrists, and like all mothers everywhere, they once in a while twirled before us in the living room, perfumed and teased, and asked us,* How do I look? *before heading out to the bar with the girls. They measured out the years and months they had been with or without a man to just about anyone who would listen, and the proximity of those men, who may or may not have been our fathers, their aggressive sexuality, loomed over our adolescence . . . But types, types . . ." he says. The monologue ends.*

Sal floats his arm through the bar to the music.

"And what's he thinking then? What's his mood?"

"Oh, I don't know, Juan. I suppose a part of him is embarrassed at his own sentimentality, and another part is thinking: *How can you blame a person for needing love?*"

Back in the bar, Norwood, still teasing, says, "Something happened to them. Something happened to you."

The elderly fellow groans. "For God's sake," he says, but he stays right there on his stool.

Norwood orders four shots of tequila, one for every person left in the bar, including the bartender.

"*Last call was twenty minutes ago. Bar's closed,*" the bartender says. *But he pours them.*

The camera looks through the bar window, to the street outside, where the people move in time to the music playing inside, music they cannot hear. They stumble, they bark and slap backs, but the music makes them graceful, fluid, as if in some kind of choreographed dance, as if submerged in the music, floating gently among the rhythms.

Then a hard, abrupt cut, the opposite shot, the camera is outside on the street looking in through the window. The music cuts short. We hear only the aggressive noises of the night: the bars emptying, honks, shouts, the bass from a passing car. There's the kid, a teenage hooker, an eel among the tortoises. Some men on the street turn their heads as they pass by the window and they smirk at the kid, the same way the girls' mothers had.

Then we're back in the bar, where the kid is fighting a battle inside himself: whether and how to keep his dignity. There's too much to tell, to confess, too many bars with old men, hungry for a certain kind of story wrapped up in a nubile package. We sense this from the way he looks up at the angled mirror above the bar, and there in the reflection is the river.

Cut to a flashback. One of the girls says to the kid, "You walk around with this huge fucking neon sign above your head and this arrow pointing down at you, like those signs in front of motels that say ROOMS AVAILABLE, *except your sign says* SOMETHING TERRIBLE HAPPENED TO ME, *and you keep that sign all lit up like that above you, and you want people to ask, you want the whole fucking world to feel sorry for you, but no matter how much you tell it, no one's ever going to understand, and it's never going to be enough."*

To which the kid replies, "I've been fucking these guys."

For a moment, no one speaks. Then one girl laughs, another nods. They're all high.

"For money. I've been saving up."

The rain falls and dimples their little river—the kid wants to move on, but he's trapped there, by their side. He keeps looking and looking at the river.

"Oh, shit, and I forgot another scene, from a while back, where the kid finally goes down to the clinic; he has a disease. Norwood is bound to find out."

"What was the scene?"

"Let's see, it's just Sal and the clinic nurse, or counselor, or whatever, a young guy, and he's asking the kid how he thinks his partner will react. He's asking with a bit of the routine distance, but also kindness. Sal makes a joke of it. *Oh, he won't beat me,* he says. *Just probably pack up my duffel bag and toss it down the stairs.*"

"Ah yes, the brat from the second act."

"The nurse doesn't find him funny, either, but Sal stays with the bit, pretending to get emotional. *Who's going to love me then?*"

"Let's move on."

Interior: The Glass Coffin. The kid wants to move on. Norwood's hand is on his arm, just under the armpit, in a way the kid's father used to pull him.

"Hey, G. You in a trance or something?"

He does not look at Norwood's face; he looks into the river.

"Shots!"

Sal and the elderly fellow, the bartender, and Norwood, they lick the skin between thumb and pointer and sprinkle it with salt. They take up their limes.

"After this, I'll tell you the truth," he says. "I'll tell you a true story."

Who doesn't want to be lovely, to be someone worth protecting? The window, the girls gathered at the river, the flashy dressers, the bar below and the future forward, bits of his own reflection, all glimmer in the angled mirror.

And then the film ends without anyone saying another word. We follow Norwood and Sal out of the bar, down the street, back up the stairs, to the attic, where the kid puts on the diaper and baby-cries.

"For him?"

"Yes, Juan. For him."

Starve a rat today.

New York City Department of Health

But, nene, where did the film's title come from?"

"Right, sorry. Remember in the beginning, when the boy is walking on the beach with his father, and we can't hear the questions, but we can hear the father's answers? Well, the last thing the father says is that in Brooklyn, in Gowanus, around the projects where the father grew up, there were these signs, all over, reminding people not to be sloppy, to cover their garbage. The signs read: STARVE A RAT TODAY. And the point was this: you could judge a man by the company he kept, and if you talk a lot of trash, you attract a lot of rats, and what kind of boy was he? And what kind of man did he want to become? And the kid best learn how to keep a secret."

███
███
███
███████████████████

Résumé:

████████ Tendency to femininity ███████████████████████.
Mother dominates father.

██████████. Attached to mother. Helped her ███████████ Called
sissy. ████████████████████████

██
██ nauseating.

██
███████ decidedly ██████████████.

████████. Homosexual██████████████████████████████
███████████████████████████████

DENNIS C.

General impression:

On a hot afternoon ████████ Dennis comes ██████████████ neatly
████████████████████████████████ with prominent ████████
████████████████ trousers, apparently unaware of the ████████
████████████ mincing ████████ rotatory swaying of his hips██
████████ coy ██████████████████████████and unclear,████
████████████ why he has always been called.████ Nevertheless ███████████████████████████████ he is delicate and
chivalrous ████████████████████████ he permits ██████████
freer play ████████████████████████ the gayest of the "queens."

Dennis has a gracile body ███████████████████████████████
████████████████████████████████████ his embarrassment.
His capacity for grace █████████████████████████████████████
██████████ the small, but firm ████████████████████████
████████████████████ pink cheeks ██████████████████████
██████████ long lashes ██████████████████████████████
█████████████████ health ██████████ in his face, a little
more than might be expected ███████████████. It is probable also
that ████████ an old lover ████████████████████████████.
█████████████████████ of his youthful zest.

█████████

████████████████████████████████████ Protest██

V

EL CALDERO

and the Queen, the Witch who lights her fire
in the earthen pot, will never tell us what she knows,
and what we do not know.

— **ARTHUR RIMBAUD,** "After the Flood"

Through research, Juan had managed to find out both women's birth names: Zhenya Gay had once been Eleanor Byrnes, and Jan Gay was born Helen Reitman. From there he was able to order up microfiche rolls, where he found small mentions in the local papers, though only about Jan. His sense of Zhenya he gathered from studying the children's books themselves for moments of autobiographical revelation captured in code in the words and drawings; little scenes of erotic discovery through which the queer child stumbles upon unbidden knowledge of the self.

"Oh, you mean squirrel, you!" squeaked Carolyn. "I'll pull your tail and I'll pull your ear, too, you silly squirrel, you!" And she did.

And then Sarah and Carolyn really lost their tempers. There was a great deal of pulling and squeaking and chattering. Even bits of fur floated about. Suddenly Sarah and Carolyn stopped quarreling and just looked at each other. Then they ran to their homes, Sarah up the tree and Carolyn into the tiny hole in the ground.

As Helen and Eleanor, the two met in 1927, the same year Juan was born. After a very brief courtship they were privately, surreptitiously "married." Eleanor briefly took on Helen's last name, Reitman, before both decided they needed more radical reinvention, and so Eleanor Byrnes became Zhenya Gay, and Helen Reitman became Jan Gay.

Zhenya is a Russian diminutive, a nickname without a fixed gender. The name *Jan*—much like *Lesley*—has, over time, shifted in its gender connotation. In the time and place of her childhood— that is, the early twentieth-century Midwest—*Jan* was more often a man's name, the Scandinavian equivalent of John (pronounced *Yahn*).

While the pair traveled around the Caribbean and Central America, they cowrote their first children's book, about a little brown boy, titled *Pancho and His Burro*. Others followed, including one Zhenya wrote with another woman, a painter, titled *Manuelito of Costa Rica*. Zhenya's brilliant illustrations carried all the books and saw them to publication; Jan contributed to the narratives; and Juan served as model. The couple loved imagining other lives for this child, their charge, whom Zhenya had found on the street in San Juan, lost in a dream, and whose parents had entrusted the boy into their care as he made his way from the island to live with relatives in the States; an ethereal boy who had been briefly, affectingly, their own.

One advantage of choosing ambiguously gendered names was that, on paper—on the manifest of the honeymoon cruise the couple took to the Caribbean, say, or on the covers of the many books they cowrote—their names could appear side by side and announce a relation that might be spousal or otherwise. They stayed in the Caribbean longer than they'd expected, and for the purposes of the journey back to New York, with Juan in their care, they bestowed upon him the shared surname, Gay.

"And *gay* meant gay then as now?"

"Yes, child. To those who knew. Even if the word's other sense was still in popular use."

"And why did you keep the name? After you lost trace of them?"

"What makes you assume it wasn't they who lost trace of me? I was a child. We'd come north together, the three of us, on a passenger ship from San Juan to the New York Harbor. I imagine they paid my passage, as exchange for the modeling I'd done, though nothing was explained to me about all that, I was only told I would live with an uncle and aunt already settled in Spanish Harlem, though I can't remember if anyone was calling it Spanish Harlem in those days, or if that came later. Anyway, those tíos in Harlem had no children of their own; I'd go to school, and one day soon my mother and father and brothers and sisters and I would all be reunited, but until then I was to take my schooling very seriously."

"How old were you?"

"Young. So young. Six or seven? *Master English*, they told me."

"You must have been terrified, to leave your mother, to leave everyone."

"I didn't understand enough about geography, about time and

space and distance, to truly understand. And I was so besotted with Jan and Zhenya, and with the idea of sailing the ocean . . ."

"And the little unnamed boy in the jungle, in *Who's Afraid?*, and all the other versions—Pedro, Manuelito, Pancho, Pablo— the boy whom Zhenya kept writing about and drawing, renaming and reimagining, again and again—for decades, Juan—always soft and feminine, that little boy is you?"

"They're clever drawings. Tender. Are they not?"

Did you ever pat a baby goat
And learn how soft he feels?
Did you ever watch him walk about
On his four little black high heels?

21

O kay, Juan, ready when you are. But what will you call the film?"

"*The Opening of a Door*. I've stolen the title from the book Jan was reading, when I knew her, on that sea voyage."

"You've read the book yourself?"

"Many years later, yes. Fantastically gay for its time. But my film has nothing at all to do with the plot of the book, only the title, which floated up into my mind just now, while I was lying here trying to compose Jan's story into this film for you, searching for a conceit that might hold together a rather boundless life."

Interior: Brooklyn Hospital, sometime in the early 1930s. The first image we see is a hand on a doorknob. The hand belongs to a shadowed figure, shot from behind, impossible to tell whether woman or man, no rings, no paint on the nails, only a strong, firm grip. Pull back: a man's square-shouldered jacket; pull back farther still, it's our Jan. She turns the knob and enters the office, where she is visibly struck by the air—pungent and hazed and unpleasant to breathe. Zoom in on a cigar, a Cubano, smoldering on the desk's ashtray; the camera pulls up to the doctor's face, a man in his seventies, white hair, pinkish face, white beard. He rises, but does not come out from behind the desk, only motions to a chair.

"Please," he says, "sit."

He's asked Jan to come to him at the end of the day's patients; now, sleeves rolled up, he sips from a tumbler, something amber, scotch. He does not offer to fix her a drink. Otherwise, he is exceedingly polite. Prior to the meeting, Jan gleaned only a few facts about him, in an old copy of Who's Who? *He was born 1861, founder of the National Committee on Maternal Health. Recently, he's devoted himself to the problem of female homosexuality.*

Well, here I am, Doctor, *Jan thinks,* specimen and expert both.

"And it's not a contemporary movie, looking back at history, but an actual Old Hollywood film, is that right? In black-and-white?"

"If you like."

As Jan and the Doctor continue to speak, we get a slow, panning shot around the office. On one wall hangs a large anatomical sketch of labial protrusions, framed, and, Jan must admit, rather beautiful. We pull in enough to make out the signature, plain block letters followed by a slash: DICKINSON/. Other framed sketches line the wall behind: vaginas, clitorises, hymens, nipples, vulvas. A series of sculpted plates capture the stages of labor and delivery.

"You made all these?" Jan asks.

"A passion," the doctor says.

Dickinson tells Jan he's interested in gathering evidence on the gynecology of homosexuality. He hopes to measure and sketch the genitalia of female sex variants. He believes—on the evidence of the few sketches and samples he's taken so far—that through his drawings he'll be able to demonstrate physiological differences in homosexual women and thus contribute significantly to developing theories of homosexuality's cause.

"But first, Miss Gay, I'll need to collect much more evidence."

He rambles on—it's not necessary to trace the precise nature of his theories, we are reminded only that this was an era informed by the folly for eugenics. At the moment, he's speaking to the advantages of sterilizing the poor, and yet he assures her he is considered progressive by the standards of his practice, as if she doesn't, or wouldn't, know. He tells her of the considerable risk he's taken on over the years, championing birth control, challenging the Comstock laws.

"Worse than puritanical," he says, "unscientific." He speaks admiringly of Margaret Sanger. He is an ardent supporter of both abortion and euthanasia, as well as a deeply religious man. He'll serve as vice *president of Planned Parenthood, and the logo he designs for the re-branding will take the form of a cross, and be rejected.*

We realize, from the steeliness settling into her expression, that Jan didn't come for all this. She's here for something else entirely. After some time, she interjects.

"My interest in women's sexual lives has little to do with reproduction, Doctor."

He startles, just slightly, but a wry smile creeps onto his face.

"Yes, of course, yes, of course, Miss Gay."

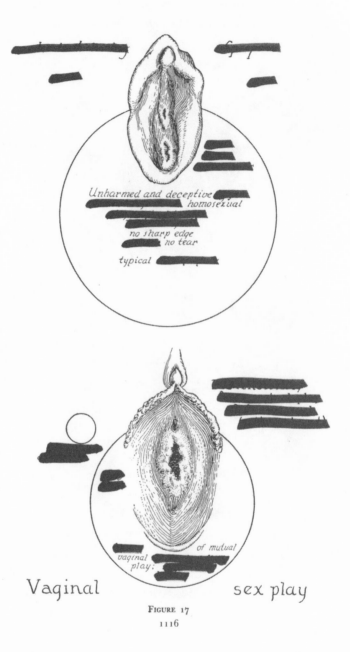

Unharmed and deceptive ~~...~~ homosexual

no sharp edge
no tear

typical

~~...~~ of mutual

vaginal
play:

Vaginal   sex play

FIGURE 17
1116

J uan?"

"Yes, child. What now?"

"What kind of film is this? Noir? Melodrama? Something blue? I can't tell."

"These interruptions—a bit hypocritical."

"Sorry, Juan, it's just that I almost can't believe you're in the room. When I close my eyes it seems the narration is coming from inside my own mind."

"A ghost story. Keep them closed."

"A ghost story. Okay, good, that's good to know. Thank you, Juan. Go on."

Dickinson seems intent, in this meeting, to make two things clear: first, his admiration for several lesbian women, and second, his conviction that homosexuality is an affliction, a disease, and that it is his responsibility, as one interested in women's sexual hygiene, to advance science in the direction of a cure, eradication.

"But do you think it a sin, Doctor?"

"It's my duty to study and to treat, not cast aspersions, Miss Gay. Though I don't go so far as some of your German doctors. I see no cause for celebration in disorder."

At some point Jan reaches into her bag and pulls out a manuscript. She tells Dickinson this is all of it, the sum total of her years of research.

The few facts she knows about Dickinson, his answers, even his attitude in that first meeting, all point to a certain ambivalence at the man's core. At this late stage in the doctor's life, Jan is surprised to find such undisguised ambition, such energy; she wonders whether he is

*insecure about his legacy. As for his attitude toward lesbians in general,
she's found what she hoped for—not empathy, nor pity, but curiosity.
Dickinson seems a curious man in every sense, and curiosity Jan can
work with. So when the doctor asks her to leave the research with him,
she does, though she hands over the pages with difficulty.*

"My only copy, Doctor."

"Well then, I promise to read with care."

Jan focuses on the wry smile. She thinks, Maybe, maybe.

"Come see me again," *he tells her.* "Same time next week." *Then we
cut to the title card:*

THE OPENING OF A DOOR

"Every scene, you see, begins with the turning of the doorknob.
The hand on the knob may be firm or timid, sometimes the hand
of a man, sometimes a woman, sometimes a child—but always
the opening of a door. And one never knows what room the door
might open onto."

"An experimental film. Very chic."

"The narrative is not chronological, nor does it stick closely to
a single character's point of view. Not only do you not know what
room the character has just entered, you don't even know the decade, until after the door has opened and you've had a moment to
adjust, to piece together the visual clues."

"But Jan is not the ghost, eh, Juan? I wouldn't like that."

"Nene, there are no ghosts just yet. But they are many. And
they're coming."

*A montage of scenes now: the arc of Dickinson's career beginning in
the late nineteenth century and moving through to the present. We see
Dickinson opening the same door, onto the same examining room, over
and over, though the patients change, and with the changing patients,*

the years advance as well. Medical evolution, reflected in the office furnishings, the fashion styles of his patients, the gynecological equipment, as well as Dickinson's manner of examination and experimentation.

The scene pitches somewhere between humor and horror—the shape and heft of the metal specula, the embryotomy spoons, the forceps, the cervical dilators, the cumbersome undergarments—and, as time marches on, where one might expect to find progress, scientific transfiguration, one finds instead transmogrification. The viewer might shudder or nervously giggle at the relative brutality of recent medical history; the viewer might think, There but for the grace of God go I. *We know a certain historical tolerance must be made for the outdated gender roles and medical ethics, but when Dickinson hides a camera in a planter in his office and secretly photographs women in the process of being examined, when he stimulates women to study their reactions, and advises a colleague it's better to have a nurse in the room, for propriety's sake, though not strictly necessary, the mood darkens.*

Another shot: Dickinson reaches for the doorknob, only it's not the examining room he enters but a separate office, where we find a very smart-looking woman in her thirties or forties, bespectacled, a doctor it seems, or an intellectual, at work amid stacks of papers and drawings. A research partner, Lura Beam—a covert lesbian herself. Jan and Lura had never met, though Jan had heard mention of her through the dyke grapevine.

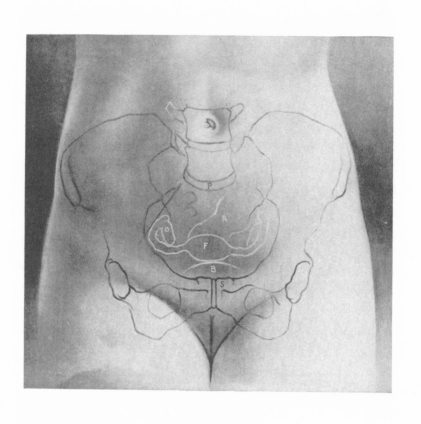

Another thing Jan can't know, at the early meeting, is how her story will be erased and overshadowed, first by Dickinson's story, and then, ultimately, by the story told by another doctor, Dr. Henry. She knows only that her research—the three hundred interviews she's conducted in London, Paris, Berlin, New York—none of it can be published without the cover of a medical doctor. A male doctor. She's tried. Everywhere. For several years now. A paradox."

"What paradox?"

"Well, Jan's story can't be told without a patriarch and yet there is no patriarch to her story. A self-made woman, abandoned by her father when she was just a toddler. And the grand irony is that her own father was himself a gynecologist, a notorious, truly radical gynecologist. The famed hobo doctor. He ministered to those who could not afford care, those whom doctors refused to see: the hobos, tramps, and whores; cirrhosis, gonorrhea, syphilis. A man respected by the radical left, though in no way respectable. He was the great passion of Emma Goldman's life, and was himself an advocate of free love, though he disliked lesbians, mannish, aggressive dykes especially. And Jan disliked him, resented him for walking out on her and her mother, and while she may have respected his anarchosexual ideas, what little she gleaned of his personality, she detested."

"Wait, Emma Goldman?"

"The one."

"But Juan, you're skipping around much too quickly."

"Am I? Sorry, let's see . . ."

A hand on a doorknob. Jan's hand; the door opening onto Dickinson's office. Their second meeting, though this time the meeting is more of an interview. Dickinson has read the manuscript, and he has many questions. He leans forward, smiles, listens, as Jan recounts her travels to Hirschfeld's Institut für Sexualwissenschaft; how she studied everything she could find, everything in print, surely, on lesbianism, homosexuality, inversion, hermaphroditism, sex variance—terms often used interchangeably, a bit willy-nilly—in the libraries of Berlin, and London, and Oxford; how throughout the 1920s and early 1930s, she interviewed every lesbian she could in those cities; and how she compiled the manuscript: three hundred case studies, three hundred lesbian lives, in detail.

"Scientifically speaking, I'm afraid, my dear, the manuscript is useless." Dickinson pauses, and when Jan says nothing he adds, "Folk wisdom."

Jan looks furious, but under the anger, we can tell, she is shaken.

"And yet, Doctor, I've got a publisher in London ready to bring the work out. All I require from you is the shield of a credentialed expert."

Dickinson is not at all interested in lending his good doctor's name to the cover of her book, but he is very much interested in her friends and acquaintances, her access to the deviant underground, her fearlessness. He pivots to sweet talk, tells Jan she is an asset, a formidable, clever young woman. He would like very much to find a way to work together, to benefit from her vast research, her life's work thus far. He suggests that together they put in motion the process that will result in the formation of the Committee for the Study of Sex Variants. Jan's job will be recruitment, primarily, but advisory as well, perhaps a bit of administration. In the end, she agrees. The committee will eventually break Jan, but when Dickinson comes out from behind the desk to shake Jan's hand, when he at last offers her that drink, we can tell— from the expression on Jan's face as they clink glasses—Jan believes she has finally caught a break.

The opening of a door: this time, it's Jan who sits on the other side of a desk. Her own office. Some stretch of time has passed, and the one coming through the door is Thomas, a researcher in training, someone whom Jan is apparently initiating into the study, teaching how to take case histories, using herself as a practice model.

"Read to me what you have so far," *she says.* "Begin with impressions."

"Okay, well: Miss Gay wears—"

"Jan G."

"Right, sorry, of course. Jan G wears no makeup, and this lends her face a certain distinction. An almost impolite clarity. She will not hide that she has aged, lived, suffered."

"Impolite clarity. I see you're going for poetry. And what else have you written?"

"You're making fun."

"Maybe. Maybe I like it. Go on."

"I'm trying to sound like the samples you gave me. You told me to try."

"So go on already."

"And she smells of cigarettes and warm musk. The lines and pallor of her face, the rasp of her laugh, betray a drinker's decline—both peculiar and familiar."

"So I'm a drinker?"

"Are you not?"

"I've always been bright. That's the problem . . ."

Jan points to the notebook open on the young man's lap, indicating he ought to be taking this down.

". . . Always felt every shade of meaning in the room, and so yes, I drink. But methodically—in the evenings, and all day on Sundays— to quiet my mind. My father, you see, whom I did not meet until I was grown, diagnosed my personality almost immediately after making* *my acquaintance.* You're the type who never misses a trick, *he said. And then he added,* You'll suffer for it."

Thomas puts down his pen, looks up at Jan. "They do seem to always jump right to fathers, don't they? Or mothers?"

"Well, no. It only appears that way in the record. Part of your job is to get them on to fathers and mothers; I'm just speeding things along a bit. But also, my father, you must understand, was quite a famous man. Or infamous. An infamous trickster. The last great hobo intellectual."

"Someone I've heard of?"

"No, never ask that. Too much risk of exposure. If you have heard of him, you'll remind the variant of the impossibility of true anonymity. If you haven't, you might embarrass her, make her out to be a teller of tall tales."

Thomas nods. Picks up his pen. Thinks for a minute.

"What do you think he meant, You'll suffer?"

"Well, I don't know how the comment was intended, but I can tell you it puffed me with pride. For years after, I considered never miss-ing a trick *to be the highest form of intelligence. Later, I came to re-alize the cost of believing so fully in one's powers of perception. In my daily life, at work on the committee, I swing between states of anxious hypervigilance and fantastical egoism. But at night, you see, I find myself incapable of self-delusion, incapable, even, of simple escape, so I drink and drink and still miss nothing. Only I find moments of mercy in the drink, usually around dusk, when at least I feel less.*"

"Did you ever try to quit?"

"No, no. Redirect. Don't overly fixate on the so-called moral fail-ings. You'll meet with drinkers and petty criminals, dope users, and some will be low, and some will be high-society folk. All will have been living with secrets. All will have cracked in one way or another. But don't forget that they've survived as well—and that they've had to be creative to do so. Don't forget to ask about that. Besides, every variant comes in with an agenda. If I'm willing to speak so freely about my *drinking, it may well be because I don't want you poking around into something else. Try again."*

While Jan talks, we watch the young man's face transform. The look of concentration and consternation melts away, replaced by the beatific smile of the acolyte. An idea comes to him then.

"Tell me about the work," he says.

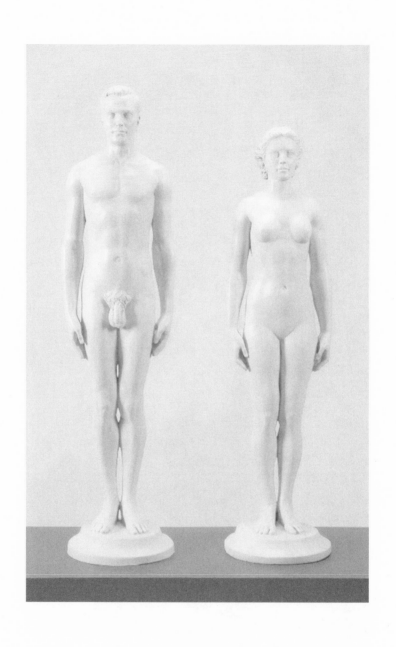

I n the beginning, within the scientific community, our work was viewed with skepticism, or else condescension. The entire committee was suspected to be packed with perverts, though I'd guess only half of us qualified. Dr. Henry is terribly straight. Dr. Dickinson believes in all sorts of nonsense about hierarchies—racial and otherwise—he's even designed these ridiculous dolls, Normman and Norma, meant to represent perfect human proportions and features. Alabaster dolls. Rubbish. Not one moment of the study would have been possible without me, but every day I feel I'm being pushed more and more to the sidelines. I used to come and go as I pleased, speak and dress and act as I'd always spoken and dressed and acted, but then Henry got it into his head that my behavior and status sowed confusion among the variants and the researchers. One day, an edict came down that disallowed trousers for women. I had to buy a skirt set. The calf-length skirt fell straight, roomy enough to require only a three-inch slit at the back—a sexless slit, to be sure—and while it does not constrict my stride, God forbid I ever need to run in the thing. When I get home, I tear it off. I'm a bit of an expert on nudism. I'm sure you've heard."

"Yes, from the others. They pass around your book, though I haven't yet seen it myself."

"Well then, Thom, something to look forward to. Anyway, to carry out the study, we were assigned an unused wing, sordid little rooms cramped with broken furniture, which we did our best to mend or clear. There was a typo in the memo authorizing the study, such and such basement rooms to be set aside as a 'palace' of observation. And that's what we've called it ever afterward: the Palace of Observation."

Wait, Juan, the Palace?"
"Now you see."

A hand on a doorknob. The hand belongs to one of the variants, Salvatore N, who opens the door and peers in, tentatively. This is a much grander office than the one in which Jan had interviewed with the trainee; and an engraved nameplate tells us the man seated behind the desk is Dr. Henry, who brusquely motions Salvatore into the room.

"Well," Henry says, "and are you going to sit?"

"Yes, yes, sorry, yes. I'm afraid I've come a bit unmoored."

The great love of Salvatore's life, an Italian dockworker, has moved back to Naples and broken Salvatore's heart. Salvatore attempts to describe the farewell scene, but Henry repeatedly steers Salvatore back to questions about sexual practices, and though Salvatore complies, it's clear that just the same, he'd rather not get too much into all that; he wants to describe the connection the two shared, above all—he wants to get that down into the record.

Salvatore is sweet, and vulnerable, and easy to love. He does not thrash about in the chair, but sits very still and attentively. He tells Henry that the dockworker had a younger sister, Nora N, and the three had lived together, not so long ago. Nora is also participating in the study.

"I think I have started her on a different life," Salvatore says. "She didn't know about homosexuality until I told her, and from that time she has opened up and blossomed. A year ago, I encouraged her to leave our home to live with a girl. She doesn't want to be cured. Since she has come to realize that she is a homosexual, she has thrown all conventions to the winds. I guess she has a notion she might as well live her life while she can."

"And you think that's unwise?"

"To live freely? If such a thing is possible, then indeed she should."

"And you?"

"Oh, I have no such notion for myself. I'd like to be cured, you see. Straightened out."

"Have you attempted intercourse with a woman?"

"I used to be in love with our family physician. I thought he might cure me, a very handsome man. You know, I would give anything to have an affair with him, and then question him about my sexual behavior."

Dr. Henry cannot help but smile; he swallows down a little laugh.

A shadow passes over Salvatore's features.

"Nothing I want, can I have," Salvatore says. "Sometimes it seems the only way out . . . well, I don't know, Doctor. I would like to be normal. I would like a husband. I'd like to live normally in an abnormal way."

"After we're done here, there will be a rather extensive physical examination. You'll need to cooperate fully."

"I understand."

Salvatore stands, takes his jacket from the back of the chair and drapes it over his arm. Henry scribbles down notes, then looks up to see Salvatore's hand stretched out across the desk, waiting to shake goodbye. For a moment, it seems Henry might refuse to take the hand, but he does, one quick shake, and then Salvatore leaves, closing the door gently behind him. Once he's gone, Henry tosses the notebook onto the desk, then turns his back to the camera and looks out the window, down to the street.

"I like it, Juan. You're very clever. But tell me, why did he pause before taking Salvatore's hand?"

"Perhaps because the doctor knew the hand would be clammy, the wrist limp, the touch much too tender . . . Or perhaps it felt dangerous to say a final goodbye to one so clearly in distress. Remember this: not all ambiguities need be resolved, nene."

The camera pans to the desk, to the notes, and we're surprised by the tone: "The future looks dark . . . thoughts of suicide but too much of a coward . . . If things go on this way there is bound to be a crash."

A hand on a doorknob. Jan arrives at home, the entire second floor loft of an old firehouse in Chelsea, on Twenty-First Street between Eighth and Ninth. The space is an enormous dance studio, with two bedrooms curtained off on either side. An illegal arrangement, surely: no kitchen, only a hot plate; an icebox in the bathroom. Jan is much older now. She finished work with the committee several years ago. A failure. No one else is around. She carefully hangs her outer clothes in the walnut wardrobe, then removes and folds her underclothes. Nude as the news, she fixes her first drink, a Manhattan. She plops in a maraschino cherry, but the old-fashioned kind, a rich black color, from the days before they started bleaching the cherries and dyeing them bright red.

Cut to the meticulous preparation of the second drink. Others are home now. From the other side of the curtained bedroom, we hear the sounds of a dance lesson. Another cut: a sloppier, third Manhattan. A montage then: Jan arriving home, getting naked, fixing drinks, pacing; sometimes she's with her girlfriend, sometimes she's in a rage, shoving guests out the door, or slamming down the telephone. Sometimes she's alone, sitting on the floor and staring fixedly at a mass of papers spread out across the coffee table, scribbling.

Her lover is Franziska Boas, a dancer, and the owner of the loft. Zhenya is long gone. Franziska and Jan are both the daughters of "great men." Jan's father is infamous. Franz Boas is eminent. The "father of American anthropology." The roommates who rent the second bedroom are Andy Warhol and Philip Pearlstein, a painter.

percussion instruments, piano, drums, ubangy and chinese records.
2. books, plants, tapestries, naked statues of franziska
Boas – the woman with whom we share
the studio with, and another lady who
writes on nudity. ~ very strange. but don't
misunderstand me. we have our own room. we share
the studio we paint and she dances.

come up any time. any time you nothing to do
its really a very arty place. real nice

i just stepped on a bug

A ndy Warhol? You're shitting me."

"I shit you not. Though he would still have been Warhola in those days. This was just after he'd moved to New York.
1949, 1950, something like that. Andy Warhola, poor and unfa-
mous. He's very much beside the point of the scene, nene. The
point is Jan. How upon arriving home, the first thing was to
neatly fold and hang her clothes in the wardrobe. This way, no
matter where the night took her, no matter how damaged she felt
in the morning, or how harried, or how late she was in getting
out the door, she had something unwrinkled to put on. How she
always drank from a glass, always rattled out the ice from the tin
tray, always splashed in vermouth, even if the temptation was to
pull the bottle of bourbon straight to her lips and suckle. How
some evenings she could slow down, become absorbed in the real
work, jotting down the day's recollections, figuring out how to
compose a response, a counternarrative to the *Sex Variants* book.
How might she undo the harm of the doctors' editorializing?
And if she slowed her thoughts, the drinking slowed as well, and
she might make it to bed without tipping over. Most nights,
though, she tipped. Into rage. Or paranoia. No friends remained
whom she might telephone—they'd only speak to her if she was
sober—and so she paced and mumbled her grievances aloud into
the room. She came home, she tripped, and she tipped."

"And how does the scene end, the montage?"

*The camera pulls away, moves outside the window. We see Jan in her
apartment, in the main room, on the dance floor, alone, with every*

[213]

light turned on. She is naked, of course, and she is dancing, quite grace-
fully, almost floating in light. The camera continues to pull back; we
see more of the building, other apartments—most of the windows are
dark, and those that are lit show sedentary couples, at the table eat-
ing, perhaps, or reading on the couch. Only Jan is moving, a silhouette
now, dancing in slow motion, and even when she falls to the floor, it's
drawn-out, very measured, and very lovely.

But, Juan, I think the film ought to show that Jan can still laugh at herself. I don't like to think she's as bitter, or defeated, as all that."

"Yes. Very good. We'll add more laughter."

"And this Franziska Boas, what was she about?"

"An interesting figure, nene, very involved in civil rights, choreographing multiracial dance pieces and offering free lessons to the poorer kids of the neighborhood. She pioneered the idea of dance therapy. Her father, a fascinating figure, sought to debunk eugenicist theories; he basically invented the idea of cultural relativism in anthropology. A mixed legacy, I'd say, with both, though at least they tried; but anyway, this is Jan's story. Where should we jump to next? Childhood?"

"Before she was Jan Gay?"

"That's right, nene, when she was someone else entirely: a child. A child called by another name, born 1902. You know, Jan made the local papers twice before the age of twenty, both just informational community blips, but both illustrative, both queer. One mention placed Jan among a handful who had joined the newly formed Women's Rifle Club. The other mentioned that at an upcoming YWCA meetup on Women in the Bible, *Helen Reitman will tell the story of Ruth. Meeting to be followed by a spread . . .* Only two spare mentions in the local rags, but already the image begins to emerge, the portrait of Jan Gay as a young one, rifle slung across her shoulder, Ruth chapter and verse torn from the Bible, folded into a square, and tucked down into her pocket, like a talisman—charmed and armed for the battle ahead."

"I don't know the story of Ruth, Juan."

"Well, nene, in the Bible, Ruth is Naomi's daughter-in-law, but also Ruth and Naomi are lovers. Widows. You see, first Naomi's husband died, then Ruth's, and with both husbands dead, something deepened between the two, or just as likely the affair started before their husbands passed. The Hebrew word for *cleave*, which is used to describe the bond between both Ruth and Naomi, is the same one used to describe the bond between Adam and Eve. Orpah, Ruth's sister, is married to another of Naomi's sons. He dies. All the men of all the generations are dead at this point. Naomi tries to turn Ruth and Orpah out from the home, knowing their safest bet for financial security is to take to the road and find new husbands while they're still young. Orpah protests, gently, politely, then shrugs and sets off on the road to find a suitable Moabite man. But not Ruth. *Entreat me not to leave you*, Ruth pleads to Naomi, *or to turn back from following after you; for wherever you go, I will go; and wherever you lodge, I will lodge. Your people shall be my people, and your God, my God. Where you die, I will die, and there will I be buried. The Lord do so to me, and more also, if anything but death parts you and me.*"

"Entreat me not to leave you."

"Ruth's vow is often used by straight couples, as part of their nuptials. The story of Ruth and Naomi is perhaps the first lesbian desire in literature, predating even Sappho."

"And Jan, she recognized that, caught that, when she was still so young? How?"

"A rose is a rose is a rose, and she knew what she knew what she knew."

"Tell me something about her mother. Make it terrible."

Interior: Jan's childhood home. A young child's hand on the door-knob. The door opens onto a parlor, where Jan's mother sits practic-ing at the Steinway. You can tell, from her erect posture and the purity and precision of the music, she's had formal training to be a concert pianist. Jan, just a girl, enters the room, walks to the side of the piano; she likes to stand on tiptoes and peer down inside, watching the felted hammers pound away. We understand, from the way the mother takes no notice of her, that this is allowed, a regular routine, but today, a freak occurrence: a piano wire snaps free and rips through the flesh of Jan's cheek, just under the eye. The child screams, once and quickly, then falls to the floor holding her face. Mother goes to pieces at the thought she might have blinded her daughter, but then Mother is always going to pieces. Oma, Jan's grandmother—stout and German and Catholic—rushes in, whisks Jan away to get a look. In a soothing tone she explains about tensile stress, blames the tuner for winding the strings too tightly, while over Jan's head, she chastises Mother for carrying on, this near hysteria, and she curses the girl's father, for destroying Mother's nerves.

All at once Jan understands something about Mother, not entirely in words or images, but some childish combination of the two, which has to do with nerve wires, all wound much too tightly, snapping one by one. My father, the tuner, *are the words she thinks. And then an image of Mother, helpless before the wrench.*

"And how do we see all that—the nerve wires, the father—in the film?"

"However you need to, nene. Perhaps some Buñuel-like pas-tiche: the father literally walks in, dressed as a piano tuner, applies the wrench to the mother, while grandmother and child watch in horror? However you need to see it, see it. Only do stop interrupting."

"But wait, the grandmother, what's she like?"

"For Jan, Grandmother is the idealized feminine archetype: tough and arid. *Why don't you ever cry, Oma?* Jan asks, and the grandmother shrugs. *Better to keep dry.*"

Interior: a lunatic asylum in Leipzig, in 1902. The door opens onto a ward where Jan's mother, a very young woman, has been committed. She is pregnant with Jan and has just begun the first pains of labor. Nurses rush to her side. In German, they call for the doctor. Jan's mother barely speaks the language. She is from the Midwest. She has been left stranded by her husband in a foreign land, and the stress has driven her mad. They had been on their honeymoon. They had fought, and then he simply disappeared, gallivanting across the Continent, wild and free. Mother had collapsed from shock. Her soul collapsed. This all occurred seven, eight months earlier, before she even knew she was pregnant, and now here she finds herself, giving birth in a madhouse. The usual cinematic screams. The pushing. The sound of infant Jan's wailing, brand-new voice.

Interior: a lunatic asylum in Leipzig, in 1903. A hand on a doorknob. Mother's room. It's Father, Mr. Ben Reitman, coming through the door. He has been persuaded to come back—from Prague, or Paris, or Amsterdam, or Madrid, or wherever he had fled—to return for mother and child. He pulls his hat into his hand, sheepish. Mother looks wild. The child stirs in the bassinet. The three will return to the Midwest, crossing the Atlantic in third class, all the money spent. By the time Jan is two years old, he's gone again, this time for good.

Father walks out on the family and into infamy. Over the years, as his notoriety grows, the news filters in, no matter what they try to keep from Jan. Father is an anarchist. Father is a tramp. Father is the king of the hobos. Father rode the rails for years and years. So Jan learns the hobo lingo. One day, she means to catch up with him, impress him with all she's figured out on her own. She learns the names for all the types of degenerates, and likes to play them over in her mind: "those . . . lurking in the railroad yards, pounding on back doors . . . ding-bats, old professional tramp beggars, putting on the touch; the elderly stew bums wasting themselves on rot booze; jack-rollers, sneaking around lumber and mining camps, angling for wallets on paydays; road yeggs, planning safe-blowing jobs and gang holdups; mushfakirs, their umbrella-mending kits strapped to their shoulders, looking for honest work; gandy dancers; hobo shovel stiffs . . . young, tenderfoot gay cats, new to the road and its perils; pathetic jungle buzzards, feeding off the leavings after hobo feasts . . ."

During puberty Jan lies prone, clamps a pillow between her thighs, and grinds her pelvis into the mattress, while fantasizing about Emma Goldman. (Later, she'll laugh, thinking about this, her first crush.)

She knows Father and Emma Goldman are lovers, have been for many years. My handsome brute, *Emma calls him. When Emma crosses the country advocating for free speech, or birth control, or the dismantling of capitalism—Father is not just in her entourage, he's by her side, and in her bed.*

I dedicate this book

TO

EMMA GOLDMAN,

THE MOST BRILLIANT AND MOST USEFUL WOMAN
I HAVE EVER MET.
SHE TAUGHT ME THAT MEN AND WOMEN WOULD
NEVER BE FREE TILL THEY LEARNED NOT
TO EXPLOIT NOR BE EXPLOITED.

J an's *first encounter with the word* homosexual *comes from Emma, who speaks about free love and dignity for homosexuals—which no one did at the time, no one in America, and barely anyone anywhere else. She knows Father warms up the audiences before Emma steps onstage; Emma moves the masses toward a radical reenvisioning of their own lives, moves them closer to their own sense of outrage. A man walked out of one of Emma's rallies and shot the president of the United States. To death. The assassin said Emma Goldman had lit a fire inside him. Jan knows that feeling. In the streets, Emma calls for free love, but years later, Jan will find out that when it came to Father, Emma had found herself jealous, possessive. The two were hounded by the law, and often thrown in jail.* Pinched *is the hobo word.*

Down at the free public library, with a satchel of books to return, the librarian might say to Jan, Well now, young lady, I suppose you'll want to look at the newspapers? *And that will be the signal that there's been a mention of Father—in the* Columbia Gazette, *or one of the papers from Chicago or St. Louis—and the librarian will lead Jan over to the reading room and place the paper down in front of her, folded to the page. The articles are mostly about Emma, but a few are squarely about him, and there he'll come alive, ink and pulp,* Ben Reitman. *Jan rubs the stain of his name into the tip of her finger.*

G randmother dies, 1922. Jan is twenty years old. She finds a newspaper clipping, one which obviously had been kept from her, dating back to 1912, folded into one of Oma's German books, and there she reads how, in San Diego, a sheriff kidnapped Father and brought him out forty miles into the desert, in the night, in the dark. A mob waited around a fire. Father was forced from the car onto his knees, in the sand and the dust and the beam of the automobile's searchlight. They tore off his clothes. Naked, the men committed upon him "fiendish gross barbaric acts the details of which are unfit to tell." Sodomy, Jan knows. She is a smart, worldly young woman, already attuned to the complexity of sexual codes, already determined to decode them all.

Father begged the men to kill him, but they wanted him to live to spread the word. One man, a detective, pushed his face against Father's. Ordinarily we are just businessmen, doctors, lawyers. Tonight we're thugs. They burned Father with cigars; he was tarred and stuck with desert grasses and cactuses, ordered to sing "The Star-Spangled Banner" and struck for every failed note. Father told it all to the papers. "I stood naked in a yellow circle of white men who advanced in pairs, their eyes glittering in the searchlights to inflict pain. . . . One asked me if I believed in God. I replied that no God could permit such desperate deeds. Each of the fourteen stepped forward and propounded a question. I answered truthfully and they smashed me in the face as I spoke." An American flag was thrust into Father's throat until he strangled. When they finished, they gave him twenty dollars, his underwear, and a message for Emma that she *faced the same should she ever return to San Diego. They left him in the desert to find his way.*

Jan had come across other quotes from Father in the papers before; they had been brief, strident, dogmatic. Here he's quoted at length, and human. She reads all she can about the free speech fight in San Diego—a notorious battle in what seems to be an endless class war. She finds photos of bandaged men. Reads of a woman named Juanita who walked directly into police water hoses, and was dubbed a modern-day Joan of Arc. Reads of how the Wobblies was the only organization not to discriminate on the basis of color in seeking new membership—and tries to see Father there, beaten and bruised, at the center of it all. She keeps the article, already yellowing, folded into a tight square and tucked into her wallet. "What am I going to do now?" Father had asked.

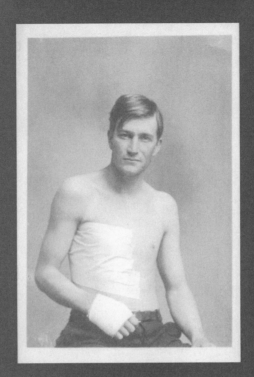

The affair between Emma and Jan Gay's father ends when one of his other lovers becomes pregnant. He had children with at least four women, three of whom it seems he married at one point or another. He is something of a folk hero who, as the story goes, conned his way into medical school. At any rate, he went from tramping to becoming a doctor. A bacteriologist. The hobo doctor. He wrote a book about pimps, *The Second Oldest Profession*. It's somewhere in this room, in one of the piles. He wrote a book about a hobo woman named Boxcar Bertha, an as-told-to autobiography. A book that, many decades later, nene, Martin Scorsese adapted into a spectacularly bad film."

"You're shitting me."

"I am not. And in Chicago, he founded a hobo college, the largest of its kind. All this and more. A large man, the son of Russian Jews, seductive, sexy. He knew firsthand the punitive treatment inflicted upon the destitute who sought shelter or care from the state. He called on hobos to look after one another; his motto was *Kindness with no red tape*."

"Does he ever come back for Jan?"

"Once or twice a letter, when she's very young, but as she grows older, no letters at all. But the mentions of Father in the paper increase, news of the work he's doing in Chicago, of his legendary life. Each new article like a shadow suddenly falling across her lap. And she feels rage, and thrill, and wonder."

"You realize, nene, I've forgotten to tell it like a film. I dropped the conceit somewhere along the way."

"I know, Juan. But I see her. Maybe I see her even better this way."

"Well, let us return to the cinematic for just a moment. Picture one of those swirling newspapers, in black-and-white, the headline snapping into focus: BLOOD WILL TELL—BE IT HOBO OR BLUE. *Helen Reitman, Missouri University journalism school coed, wearing male attire, 'rode the rods' into Chicago Friday on a Santa Fe freight train . . .*"

"Read out in an old-fashioned newsman's voice?"

"That's right. One of the many articles written about Jan's journey to go and seek him out, her father. It's impressive just how widely the story spread, picked up by papers across the country. Though I suppose the image hits at something oedipal, revelatory. Her father had not laid eyes on her in eighteen years, and then there she was, dressed as a man, dressed as him, his hobo self; the return of the repressed. For Reitman, it would have felt like seeing a ghost, the uncanny familiarity of her face; he would have wondered if she'd come to absolve, or recriminate."

"Jan's father was not hard to locate. His hobo college was the largest in the country; people came from all corners to listen to itinerants and whores, pimps and professors, deliver lectures on their various areas of expertise. Magnus Hirschfeld himself visited.

Back then the word *hobo* was often conflated with *tramp* and *bum*, though not among the working poor and destitute themselves. Over time, that flattening has worsened, and the sense and image brought to mind is of a benign, perhaps clownish, certainly archaic, form of homeless vagrant. The hobos Jan met through Father were migrant workers; most were not homeless, but forced into transience, chasing seasonal labor. Many were recent immigrants, from Greece and Italy and Ireland and England and Poland and Russia. Many were Black, part of the Great Migration. Today's analogue might be the many migrant farm workers from Mexico and Central America."

"One thing Jan could not help but notice, years later, when working for the committee, was how much her methods, if not her interests, overlapped with those of her father. His book on pimps, *The Second Oldest Profession*, ends with a series of case studies in which he transcribes the testimonies of those rarely allowed to speak in their own voices. Father grew up poor, with a single mother, a tramp—by fourteen he was riding the rails. He grew up among the pimps and the prostitutes, and then he ministered to them. Like Jan, he sought to give voice to the stigmatized, to cut through the sensationalism and provide a counternarrative. In 'Chapter X: White Girls Tell Why They Have Negro Pimps,' the reasons given by Pauline, Ada, and Pansy is that their pimps treat them well, better than white pimps they've had, or simply: *I love him and I know he loves me.*"

J an must have begun her own project, documenting lesbian lives, with something of the same hope and ambition her father had for his book; and in the early days, working with Henry and Dickinson and the others, she would have undertaken the work with excitement, the recruiting and the interviewing and the transcribing, pulling in everyone she knew. But all ends in bitterness. She writes a letter to the committee, which begins: *Gentlemen: After a careful reading of Dr. George W. Henry's manuscript of case histories based on the study of a group of homosexual men and women of my acquaintance, I beg to say that my chief reaction is one of disappointment . . . Any evangelist can moralize and call his hearers 'social outcasts.' Any social worker . . .*"

"What is it, Juan? Suddenly you look so . . ."

"Nothing, nene. Tired, is all."

"Will you go on? Any social worker, what? I want to hear the rest . . . I suppose there was not much she could really do, at that point?"

"Actually, let's leave her be."

"For good? That's it?"

"But you know the rest. Really, you do. Why don't you tell me about your Liam; it's time to let him go as well."

"Is that what we're doing?"

"Tell me about the end first, the last time you saw him. Then take me to the beginning."

"Okay, Juan. The end. I'd like that."

"And niño? . . . Try to turn me on."

"I thought you'd never ask."

I am twenty-seven years old and Liam is twenty-seven years old and he reads to me from a book about gardening. He says I can crash with him for a day, or two, or three at most, as long as I am clear we are never reconciling. *We're apart now*, he says, *forever*. I feel this. The way he pushes his hips back harder against me, forces more of me inside him. This is better, for me at least— more transactional. Over the years of our relationship, we've had sex-sex, ambitious and acrobatic, less than we should have, less than everyone supposed boys like us must, and that was down to me, my hang-ups, the blackouts, which Liam did not push. If these are to be our last fucks, we both want our money's worth, something to remember. In time, Liam finishes, but I'm too much in my head, and so I give up.

Afterward, we lie together and he explains about squash, about their seeds. Sometimes, afterward especially, I like very much to be explained to, to listen. He knows the strangest things, about heirlooms and heritages and invasive species.

We nap, wake, horny again. The permanence of our split acts as an aphrodisiac. One of Liam's jobs is with the city, part-time, landscaping the parks; he's not allowed to work shirtless and so has cropped the sleeves off his assigned T-shirt. The result is the starkest farmer's tan I've ever seen; a pale Ken doll whose arms and face have been swapped out with another, darker Ken. I find this impossibly sexy—*dismembered* is the word that plays in my mind. I push my nose into his pits. He rolls onto his back, and I lick and spit, and once inside, I focus on the tan line at the base of his neck, everything above warm and angry; cool and smooth below. *Beheaded*, I think. *Reheaded. Headed nowhere.*

When he finally slips out of bed, he puts on a record, Roberta Flack's cover of "Hey, That's No Way to Say Goodbye," which might seem overly dramatic, but honestly, when we were together, he played it every morning and it did not feel portentous, simply our waking-up and leave-taking song. I watch him as he dresses for work. He keeps a second job washing dishes at a music hall downtown. Liam himself is a musician. Tonight, there's a band he wants me to see, a band he knows I'll like, because Liam does indeed know me, my tastes, especially in music. So the plan is I'll go down and stand in the back alley, smoking cigarettes, until Liam comes out to prop open the door, and then I'll follow him back through the kitchen, and the two of us will emerge on the side of the stage; I'll slip into the crowd at the front, while he heads back to work.

Liam searches for some accessory on the closet floor, suspenders probably.

"Do you need money?" he asks.

And although I'm about to make a hundred bucks for letting some wealthy dude massage and suck me off, I know this will infuriate Liam. Not that he's a puritan, but I'm careful not to remind him of all the lies I told when we were together. So I need to say yes to the money he offers, if I'm to cover my tracks. I feel shame, but distantly, dully, and the feeling is essentially narcissistic; what I ought to feel is guilt. I pretend not to hear.

Liam is that rare white boy who never goes red in the sun, only golden; over the course of summer, his brown hair lightens to sand to match his eyes, and it's gold, gold, gold, all the way down. He has a thick, healthy cock. In bed he is never goofy, but hungry, whereas out of bed he's happy to be goofy. I'm always hungry, and often angry, and covetous, and in bed, especially inwardly, I feel a kind of detached disdain, though I'm an expert at hiding all of that, and I hide it for Liam's sake, or at least I tell myself it's for his sake, to protect him, and this is one self-justification for the whole prostitution thing, a kind of steam release, where I can at least be myself and hate the sex I need.

"Do you need money?" Liam asks again.

"Only to eat," I answer. "And we're—you're—out of toilet paper. And drugs."

He laughs and hands me a wad of ones, which are still in his work pants from the night before; at shift's end, the waitresses come into the kitchen and tip Liam out. He's had and enjoyed sex with girls in the past, girls who loved him, and I used to imagine all the waitresses were also in love with him, and a jealousy would flare up inside me at the image of these girls counting dollar bills into his outstretched palm. Of course nowadays, I see the connection with the erotic charge, the feeling of value I get when older men count out twenties into my own palm.

Now it's "The First Time Ever I Saw Your Face," and Liam pokes his head back into the room, and we sing together: *I felt the earth move in my hand / like the trembling heart of a captive bird / that was there at my command.* We love that line, the absurdity of the mixed metaphor, what the hell is it supposed to mean? And we love especially the way Roberta begins on a high shout and then drops to a softer, lower register.

I t's not easy, feeling my way backward."

"Take courage. Think of Lot's wife, leaving Sodom. How she dared to turned back."

"Wasn't she turned into a pillar of salt?"

"You don't think she knew that would happen? She'd heard God's warning. Nene, *she looked anyway.*"

"Why?"

"Well, what do you think she saw?"

"Suffering? The fires. The wrath of angels."

"And how awesome the destruction. No? From a certain distance, the catastrophic must be indistinguishable from the sublime."

"And Jan's story, does it end in some kind of backward glance?"

"Maybe. Maybe for Jan, it ends in a blackout."

"Nothing I've seen compares to all that."

"No, of course not. But just count down, look backward, then look back further still, and see where you end up."

3.

I spot a golden feather on the cement edge of the platform, waiting for me, while I myself wait for the train. I think of a joke, about rats devouring an entire golden pigeon—but there's no one around to share the joke with. A bum expertly sleeps on a too-small bench, a woman pulls herself inward, stands far away, and watches her toes, and a very young man gives me a very rough look. I pluck up the feather, which is on a thin chain, but stay squatted there close to the edge, leaning my head into the danger zone. I can see all the way to the next station, where the train idles, headlights like tiger eyes in the tunnel jungle. I wait there, poised, fascinated, as the train approaches and the tiger eyes widen. When I finally snap out of it and stand, the woman and the young man are staring baldly. We're all connected, all relieved that I will not jump. I dangle my feather for them on its chain, as if to explain myself, all of this in just a blink of a moment, then the train roars its arrival, doors open, and we step into separate cars. It's late, past midnight, and I'm headed uptown to clean for a man.

The man lives in the penthouse suite of a building overlooking Central Park. There's a doorman whom I must tell my name and the name of the man I'm there to see. I use a made-up name for myself: Salvatore. The doorman introduces himself as Freddy and gives me a wink, a light-skinned Black man, likely in his fifties.

"You Latin?"

"Puerto Rican," I say, pushing my hands into my back pockets and puffing out my chest.

"Yeah," says Freddy, grinning. "Course you are."

On my way to the elevator Freddy calls after me to come back. I come and stand before him, and Freddy makes a motion to suggest that I come even closer, as what he has to say is only for me to hear, though we're alone in the lobby.

"You line up all the skinny little brown boys I seen pass through this door, headed exactly where you're headed"—Freddy leans farther in my direction—"you line them up and you know what you'd have?"

I wait.

"What do you think you'd have?"

I let my gaze crawl down to Freddy's crotch, over his little desk, his crumpled sports-car magazine, then slowly back up to his creased face, his smugly mischievous eyes. I look at him patiently and deliberately.

"You'd have the army of a third-world country," Freddy says, and breaks into squawks of laughter.

When I get to the apartment the man instructs me to keep my underwear on. The apartment is open and very modern—sixteen-foot ceilings and one wall somehow entirely made of glass.

I move along the window-wall, polishing with ammonia and newspaper. I like the reflection of myself in the nighttime glass, the way my body is almost translucent, its borders and features only hinted at, and the way the city lights and the black-green hole of the park are contained within, and spilling out of, me. The reflection of my white cotton underwear nears opacity, realness, and the gold chain with the gold feather hangs just below the gold crucifix, glimmering. The man passes comment on all the usual parts of my body, but the unusual as well—my calves, the top notch of my spine. To comment is not necessarily to compliment; of this we are both aware.

I do not look at him. I look at me in the window: half-disappeared, slim and young. I move with a cocksure air. If you don't pretend at vanity, the men feel dissatisfied. *Look at my smooth skin, look at my young face, look at my golden feather!*

And then something else, conviction, takes over; I am a very good pretender. So more than anything I want to say this: in that moment I am happy.

2.

"Explain, explain," demands Liam, but he does not want me to explain anything. I have become a monster to him, and he needs me to stay a monster. I keep silent, slowly spinning a sugar packet in a circle on the table with the tip of my finger. The waitress gives us a very wide berth—Liam weeps openly—but still, I wish she would come and refill my empty cup. I listen to Liam; I watch him cry; I rummage around inside myself and try to find a memory, a hurt, that would enable me to cry as well. I've been a dick, dicked around, the long near-decade of our relationship, countless men, often, though not always, for money—so in penance I want to cry for him now, to give him that. I rummage and rummage, but I'm dry. And besides, to trick myself into crying, to trick him, would just be another dishonesty, and I'm attempting to come clean.

"Explain!" Liam demands. He smacks the table. A grown man, blubbering like he is, and that pink thrift-store oxford with the elbows patched over, and his foppish hair—we look very gay, and a little pathetic. I can perceive us from the eyes of the round family in the neighboring booth; I can hear the thoughts of the single men, eating alone at the counter, their hunched slabs of backs to us; and the waitress, of course, I've got her number, she's never going to bring that pot of coffee around again. We look ridiculous, he especially. I should be able to shut that off, that judgment, that concern for appearances. I should look at Liam, only Liam, and feel something.

"Come on," I say. I slip twenty dollars out of my pocket and make sure to catch the waitress's eye as I lay it near the edge of the table—twenty dollars for two cups of coffee and being gay in an all-night working-class diner in South Brooklyn.

"Explain, explain," Liam whines.

I stand and lift his ratty old peacoat from the peg. "Put this on. Wipe your eyes. We're leaving. Here, napkin. Blow your nose."

I hand Liam his scarf, which he has knitted himself, poorly, and how proud he is of the garish colors and the holes and dropped stitches, the inelegance of it all, and how I watched him from the bed with a book many nights, knitting in the lamplight and playing records with our little fat, deaf cat on his lap, and how I had thought him beautiful, soft, cozy, and at the same time there was the dust and clutter and cat hair, and always the same records, broken in the same places, and how I would ponder what made him so soft—fear—and what he was so afraid of—me.

"Explain. I need you to explain, you asshole."

"Get up. Come on. Enough. I'll walk you home."

There's such a wind, such an icy wind wriggling into every buttonhole, and I have no hat. I'm glad for the wind; everyone walks facedown with the crowns of their heads fully forward, hands tucked up into armpits. No one looks at anyone else, or must be looked at—except I let that wind push and bite into my face, and I look at the men; even then, I look at all the men.

Our shabby little apartment is now his. Understandably, he does not want to let me up, but I tell him it's too cold to try and explain anything out on the sidewalk.

"Is that a joke? Is this a trick?" Liam asks. "Trickster, trickster. Am I a trick?"

He pushes the key into first one lock, then the next. He trembles. I do not want to have sex with him, but I know he needs me to want to have sex with him.

Inside, our cat pushes against our legs.

"She missed you," Liam says. I think to pick her up, but I'm wearing a long black wool coat and our cat is very white. I take Liam's hand and lead him toward the bedroom.

"No," he says. "Not anywhere it ever was. Here." He opens up the bathroom door and pulls the bulb's chain. "On the floor."

One only need glance at the octagons of white tile to feel a deep, hard coldness in one's bones, yet I strip, dutiful, diligent, and lay my bare back against the floor, and wait. Liam comes back with a condom; we have never used one before, not once.

"Where the hell did you get that?"

"Shut up."

"No, seriously, did you buy that? Already? Already you bought that?"

"Put it on."

I do. We proceed. Underneath me, the floor grows somehow colder and harder. As we start gathering steam, Liam puts his hands on my shoulders and lifts me, I think, for a kiss—we have not yet kissed—but instead, he slams my shoulders back down hard, and my skull meets the floor in a blinding, white-noise kind of way. It takes a few moments to realize that I'm curled on my side, cradling my head, eyes closed, the weight of Liam removed from my body. I open my eyes; Liam's left the bathroom and stands in the bedroom doorway, watching me. He looks unwell— shell-shocked, naked, clutching our cat to his chest—he looks very, very unwell.

"I'm okay," I say.

He sneers, huffs a crazy laughing huff, before kicking the bedroom door shut.

1.

I lock the doors to the bookstore and cut the music but leave the lights shining—the whole store suddenly hugely silent, the shelves picked over, in need of straightening. I turn the café chairs upside down on the tables and leave the empty register drawer hanging open to discourage the curious from taking a brick to the window. In the back, I count out the till. Once, I stole a hundred dollars from the drawer—in ones and fives—and how flushed Liam was when I kept pulling bills out of my pockets, how exasperated. How many jobs had I been fired from, or walked out on, over the years; how many long stretches of joblessness? I felt free. Always I'd felt free; Liam had never been fired, never quit abruptly, worked hard, grindingly hard, for social justice organizations, kept us in a shabby apartment in South Brooklyn, kept us in food, and cat food, and secondhand records. *People steal*, I told him. *People lie, people cheat. Eat or be eaten.* Except that he didn't steal, lie, or cheat.

Anyway, I'm in the back, counting out the till, and the phone rings. I think it's him. I'm expecting him, any minute. He is the one supposed to come and meet me after work, but it's Liam calling, from just outside.

"Poke your head out," he says. "You'll see me."

"I'm counting."

"Take a break, counting, sheesh, poke your head out, let me see you."

"I'll lose my place. Anyway, go home. I told you I had plans."

"Plans? Go home?"

"I told you, Lorena. And she just wants me, not us. You know how she gets; she'll want to get drunk, unload, and you have to work in the morning—and anyway she just wants me, not us. She said as much. It's not personal; she just feels superior to me, thinks I'm more fucked up than she is, so she can tell me—"

"There's a man," Liam says, "on a bicycle."

And I just shut up.

"There's a man, looking in the windows. He's sitting on a bicycle, looking in the windows. And I want you to tell me the truth. Is this man waiting for you?"

"Baby."

"Unbelievable," Liam whispers. And he whispers something else, some other word. Or it's the wind. Then Liam says, "He looks like a really nice guy. You unbelievable asshole."

He's not a nice guy, but yes, he knows how to look like one.

We stay on the phone; I stay in the back. Liam walks toward the train. The man on the bicycle waits. I plead and apologize and pretend I do not want to break up as much as I really do want to break up. All the while, I feel such anger; I'm so tired of apologizing. Liam was always finding discarded plants and taking them home to regenerate. Everywhere in our apartment are plants, thriving. This, too, infuriates me—and when Liam instructs me not to come home that night, when he tells me to come by the next day, while he's at work, and remove all my shit and never come home again, I think of those plants, of a space in the world without them. But the truth is there was a time when we both believed in the sunny rehabilitative force of his goodness.

"It's over," Liam says. "You're free."

0.

Liam and I take jobs as farmhands on a tiny two-acre farm down in Virginia—a sloppy, rocky field nestled into the folds of the Blue Ridge Mountains. We drive nonstop, taking turns behind the wheel. The car is Liam's, some old thing he'd scrimped for. We slowly chug up one side of a mountain, then slide down the other, recklessly, keeping our foot off the brake as long as possible, clenching the wheel with both hands, hollering at our luck, at our newfound right to do as we damn well please and to do it together. We are twenty years old, the both of us, and we've found each other.

At our first truck stop I steal a pair of driving glasses with yellow-tinted lenses and large black plastic frames. They make the whole world seem as if it were swimming through honey. Liam starts on some sensible nonsense about the serious consequences I'm gambling with, he speculates about the jails around those parts, the conditions, the prejudice and hostilities of others, but I slip the sunglasses on him while he's driving, I kiss him on the neck, I say, "Look."

And he says, "Wow, it's beautiful."

We arrive at night, on the heels of a rainstorm that's sucked away half the dirt road leading to the farmer's driveway. We keep sinking into little craters filled with standing water that splashes up onto the windshield, like driving through a car wash. It takes three passes before we find the turnoff, an unmarked path of red dirt, two parallel paths really, tire tracks, with grass growing up in the middle. Leaves and brambles close in from every side and slide against the windows. Three miles of driveway, with no light beyond the scope of our high beams, not even moonlight, no starlight, just trees and blackness so heavy and serious that we both stop talking and stretch our necks until our foreheads almost touch the windshield, trying to make sense of the tarry vastness around us.

"We just slipped off the edge of the world," Liam says.

The headlights catch a flash of sparkling eyes, some tiny face-less beast. Inside the car, the green light of the dashboard reflects off the soft white underside of Liam's chin. It looks as if the light radiates from inside him.

"What are you so afraid of?"

Liam takes his eyes from the drive for just a second to look at me. "Oh, come on. You love to pretend you're so fearless."

The farmer appears on the side of the path, shielding his eyes, a shotgun in his hands. Liam stops the car and cranks down his window.

"You'll have to leave the car here," the farmer says. He makes no excuse for the gun. "You bring a flashlight?"

He leads us to a small shack, a tilting, shingled structure with four walls and a wood-burning stove. The shack is perched on the slope of a minor mountain, about a third of the way up, with thick slabs of rock stuck under the front side, a new rock every year, to keep the house from tumbling forward and down into the fields of wild raspberries below. He explains all of this to us with wide sweeps of the flashlight. We'd first met the farmer that spring when he had opened up his land to the swarms of protest-ers descending on the capitol to protest the stranglehold of the World Bank and the International Monetary Fund on developing economies: a week of anger and messy celebration. (*Youth in its enthusiasm, eh, nene? That's right, Juan, the burning and the sing-ing.*) Liam and I had been among those scrappy idealists, camped out on the farm. We missed an entire day of protests because we were so taken with the seedlings and greenhouse and the moun-tain and the old hippie back-to-the-lander who told us charm-ing, paranoid stories and invited us back in the summer, when he could use the extra hands. Now, in the darkness, on the side of the mountain, the man seems ornery and off.

"She's wobbly," the farmer says, "she's aiming to pitch, but she'll make it through the summer."

"You're sure about that," Liam says, too timid to curve the statement into a question. I'm breathless from the hike and the weight of our belongings, trying to keep my panting quiet.

"No stars," the farmer replies. "The storm. Usually there's stars. Good night."

I can't open the door to that shack, can't describe the night we spent, the way we spent it, or that first wet morning; I can't get to all the blooming, opening, buds, flowers, fruit; I can't tell about the hives, the honey, the chicks that arrived in the mail, the summer lightning, our skin browning, the view from the mountaintop, the tumble down the mountainside, words I had never known, *zinnia*, *rototiller*, the word for calling the pigs to come and eat our slop, the skin of the pigs, the skin of my man, how he became my man, the promise and the pretending, the retelling of entire plots of movies in lieu of electricity; nor can I get to the feral dirty-white kitten, that scraggly runt of the barn litter, and the farmer's snicker that Liam'd done a thing as senseless as adopt her, ruined her by feeding her. I can't open the door to that shack.

No, we're on the slope of a minor mountain, in the dark, wondering what in hell we've signed ourselves up for, and how it's all going to play.

Do you know the difference between a confessor and a martyr?"

"Tell me."

"Well, a confessor is persecuted for his faith, tortured, but lives. A martyr is killed."

"Both are saints, is that right?"

"I'm not sure it's automatic; I think it takes some time. It has to do with miracles."

"And the way we choose to remember them?"

"The way we choose to forget—the human part."

"And which one was Jan? How shall we forget her?"

"I can't tell you, nene."

"Tell me this then, Juan: I'm never going back."

"Entreat you not to leave me? All endings are messy endings, nene. All that lies ahead is the great forgetting. The blackouts will come very quickly now. And the body . . . Nene, all ends are messy."

"Entreat me not to leave you."

December 3, 1956

Well, fool, that 's the date, and where are your
senses?

Where they've been well hidden for years, in a
spirits bottle

Aren't you, my merry, my free, going to purloin
them, ambuscade them?

Well, sirrah, no, not now. I am too beholden to
other gods

Which gods

Oh, the Catholic, the lesbian, even, if all be told,
the general, the usual

Where, then, is time, where tide? Why am I not
afraid of all these others?

Nip out and find me drink

Where time, where tide?

Go on away and let the others stay and pay and pray

and play at generalities.

Jan Gay

VI

THE CAGE OF VOICES

                    you shall hear
Them speak as voices call
In sleep; they have returned
And you must hear.
                    —HORACE GREGORY, "The Cage of Voices"

Juan is going. Others come to the door. They visit Juan at his deathbed, take up conversations. They begin midsentence. They take up conversations long left idle. They do not reveal themselves to me. Juan says the voices speak from a place neither inside nor out. Blackouts follow; Juan's memory worsens. All about us, I sense deterioration.

"Nothingness, Juan. Just nightmares."

"Unjust nightmares."

"Come, sit up a little on the pillows—you'll feel better."

"*This is more than a dream*," Juan says, reciting, "*it is something that is awake within a dream.*"

They come and tell him what they've done, and what's been done to them. Juan must hear. He cannot shut them out or shut them up. After they leave, only fragments, snippets, remain of what they've said, unattached to chronology; Juan suspects others have come and left no impression at all. They sit on the edge of the bed, or else they stand by the window and speak to Juan with their backs turned. One, Juan tells me, has such a body, all ropy muscles, and he holds Juan's hand and reminds him of the years when he would run his tongue into the earthy places, the crevices, the pits and cracks, the taste of sweat. I ask him to tell me more: What does he look like, this muscly man, what's he called? But the name and face are smudged from Juan's mind; he remembers the moisture of the man's palm, the calluses, the grip. Juan tells me that something of the old, familiar horniness floats just out of reach. For the first time in ages, Juan wakes with an erection, though without any desire to jerk off, or even touch himself. I ask him to show me; I touch him, tentative, but already he's shrinking; he's far away. "How old am I?" he asks. "What do I look like?" "Handsome," I say. "Distinguished. Hung." It's not just that Juan cannot remember the faces of his visitors, but the image of his own face as well—misplaced somewhere in the recesses of his mind. He asks me to bring the mirror, the small round mirror in the cheap polystyrene frame, only the mirror is no more, shattered just the other day, when I attempted to balance it on the sill of the window in order to shave, dryly. The bathroom down the hall—with its enameled cast-iron sinks and marble vanities—was too far away. I did not want to leave the room, to leave Juan's side, for a moment. He would soon die, follow the ghosts into the other place, and I wanted to be there at the hour of his death. I wanted to be there for him, yes, but also for myself, to slake my own macabre curiosity about what it might look and feel like: a final breath.

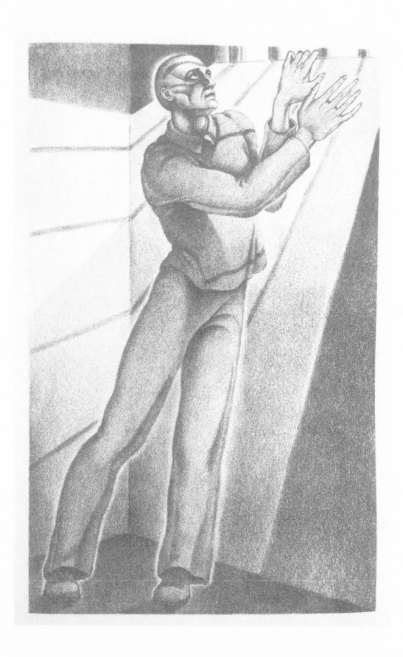

J uan is preoccupied with the others. I don't know where he goes, or where time itself goes. I lose myself, staring at the pages of a book, reading the same paragraph again and again without catching the meaning, or simply lying alongside Juan in the bed, staring at the wall, at the wallpaper, half listening for him to come around, which usually happens in the night, and then it's my turn to lead him into the trance, to elicit stories of his travels.

"Tell me, Juan, what did you see?"

"Nothing distinct, only shapes of color, impressions, but I heard the voices clearly. A woman said, *I can't tell you what to expect, only what is possible.* And then another voice, *But he can't die. He won't die.* The words repeated over and over, and a blurred form pulled into focus. It looked like my mother, blushing red all down into her neck. Splotches of red spread across her chest. I wondered what the chain she wore was about, unfamiliar to me. A gold crucifix stuck into her cleavage."

"But it wasn't your mother."

"No, right. Have I told you this before, nene? That's exactly right. I realized I was looking at another woman in the room and confusing her with Mother. The woman leaned over me, stretched to adjust something behind my head, out of my line of sight. In her movements, I sensed panic, but controlled, suppressed. Still, I felt as if my mother were nearby—I could hear her carrying on, but couldn't turn my head to look."

"You were strapped to the bed."

"Yes, yes, nene. I *have* told you this before. I wanted to know what time it was, and what day, and then I fell back down into nothingness."

"That's all you remember?"

"Of that place."

"So you died."

"Technically."

"But then you opened your eyes?"

"My eyes opened."

J uan is just below the surface; alone. He can't seem to see me, can't seem to stay up here, at the surface. I take his hands into my own, and he begins to speak, but not to me, to another, inside the dream. "Where are you?" I say, and he giggles. He mumbles something garbled, which would be unintelligible had we not grown so in tune; like a mother with her babbling toddler, I know just what he is attempting to say: *"Pull down thy vanity."* This is one of his favorite lines with which to tease me. He likes to recite the line in an absurd impression of Pound's mid-Atlantic accent, somewhere between radio broadcaster and Shakespearean bard. *"I say pull down!"* Juan's fingers are swollen and the nails are yellow. On the back of his left hand is a bruise the size and color of a plum.

J uan comes round; he gives a little shudder of horror to find me there in the room, to find himself midconversation. "I can't see," he says. "You there, in the dark." I ask him whom he's been with this time, and he tells me it was an examination, though he can't remember the details, neither what was said, nor the examiner. He'd been speaking without consciousness, and who knows what he revealed, or whose hands held his own.

"Because you could not die, would not die, and because the entire episode was very much your fault, because you sinned, and convulsed in the back of an ambulance, and your eyes rolled back until they showed only white, and you foamed at the mouth, and because you were Puerto Rican, and because reports were coming north of a strange psychiatric condition, first identified in soldiers, and because you could not be sent to jail, or banished to limbo—you were sent to this other place for observation."

"I don't understand."

"Oh, it was something like that, Juan. Don't you remember?"

"No. I want to. What time is it?"

"I know it's hard, but if only you could pay a bit better attention."

"I can feel the weight of you, sitting there, on the edge of the bed. But I can't see. I'm afraid I've forgotten your name?"

"Oh, pish, Juan. You can see. You don't need to struggle. I

share this room. I told you. Try to . . . recollect. Just sit with it a moment."

"Nene. My face."

"That's right."

Juan tells me he can hear his mother, sobbing. *No me lo quites . . .* and it doesn't feel like a memory, or a voice in his head, but as if she were here in the room, though muffled, distant. He can see another man, where he stands by the window, or the darkened shape of him. The room Juan describes is not the one we share; he says the blinds are made of crinkled paper; and that the light on the other side must be very harsh for the way the paper glows. I ask if there is a view to outside. "No," he says, "no view to outside, just the one window, which looks onto the hallway." He wonders if the muscled man will come again to perch on the edge of the bed.

"Oh, good. You're awake. Do you remember who I am? I've told you before, but you've forgotten."

"I'm sorry, dear . . . I ought to pay better attention."

"It's a muscle, Juan. Memory. It may be exercised. I think that's right . . . You told me something like that once. You know about these things better than I."

"Thom?"

"Thom's gone. Promise me you'll pay better attention."

"Gone? But he was just here. Did you see him leave?"

"Try to relax."

"He ought to have been in school that day, you know. I think he'd even started out for school, but decided instead to go see a picture show. That was his mother's wording, *picture show*. Back then he was always imitating Mother's habits of speech. This didn't make him many friends, imitating Mother. I suppose he still now prefers to say *picture show* over *movie* . . . though . . . My God. What year is it?"

"Never mind. Keep going with the story."

"And what *time* is it? I ought to rise. Get going with the day."

"Just now you were speaking of Thom. Thom at the pictures?"

"The first time. A young man sat next to him and asked if he'd ever gone with a woman."

"What was the movie?"

"Now that I don't recall—I don't think I ever knew. Silly of me not to have asked. Good for you, though. Clever. It would matter, wouldn't it? Such incidental things matter—moving images, titles, the visual detritus. They *are* the matter. I do recall Thom saying the picture dragged something awful. Melancholy. That's Mother again."

"Wait. Go slower. What's . . . the *matter*?"

"Nothing. What's the matter with you?"

"Oh, for fuck's sake."

"Did I make you laugh? Or . . . is that laughter?"

"Go on . . . tell about the movie. We like depressing films around here, don't we, Juan?"

"No, no, it was a picture show, and melancholy . . . *Daddy Long Legs*, that was the name. I must have asked after all, because there is the title, floating in front of me. And what a name . . . eh, kid? Anyway, it was melancholy and melancholia. No one spoke of depressing films or depressed people back then; depression was economic language, not personal."

"And had he ever?"

"Been depressed?"

"Gone with a woman."

"You mustn't tease poor Thom."

"How old was he?"

"Young. The man asked Thom if he'd like to try, and I'm sure Thom didn't answer but followed him nevertheless, back to his apartment. He undressed Thom and used his mouth. Thom thought at first he was going to piss and he told the young fellow to quit. The fellow said, *Just go on ahead*. It was the first time."

"So old enough to—"

"Scared Thom to death. He thought something had broke in there. He thought something was wrong with him. It made him feel nauseated. Thom went home and told an older brother, and the brother went over and gave the fellow an awful licking . . ."

"Juan."

"Yes, darling. Here am I."

"You're so . . . changed. I'm afraid I'm no good at this. I don't know how best—"

"There, there. Don't get upset. Mother will help you."

"What do you think is going to happen? After? What would you like me to . . ."

"Oh, I suppose I'll rise. It's getting late. Don't you believe I ought to rise?"

"Sure, Juan. I do."

"What day is it?"

"Your favorite question."

"There will be many questions. And all manner of tests. Poked and prodded a bit."

"But Juan, there's the matter of the . . . services . . . We never discussed, you know, arrangements . . . how you want your . . ."

"And Miss Gay is quite eager to conduct the interview. We'll have to practice your story next."

"Miss Gay. You mean Jan?"

"Now, that's very well remembered. But anyway, that's not her real surname. Imagine! Plus, she fancies herself more one of them than one of us."

"I wish I could follow."

"Oh, but you mustn't try and do that. Promise you won't try anything like that. Now. Don't you think we ought to rise? Eh, nene? It's getting late. Lost time is never found again."

Through the deep I hear shuffling sounds. Someone moves about the room, opening and closing drawers, then out into the long hallway. The air smells of, what, some kind of antiseptic? Plastic? A chemical smell, a chemical taste, there at the back of my throat. The sound of footsteps, both retreating and somehow getting louder. The noise goes through me.

I am below the surface; I am alone in the room. I wonder, where is the old man, whose name is now just out of my mind's reach, my roommate? The bed is made with hospital precision, the sheets and linens all cleaned and wrapped tightly around the mattress. I don't know what that means, if it's possible the old man has checked out for good. The light glowing through the paper blinds never alters, never wavers in intensity. I look desperately for signs of time's passing; there's no way to tell.

But then I wake, and Juan lies just as he always lies, in the bed, and ever so gentle.

T he woman begins with my feet. *Relax now*, she says. *We'll get you nice and clean for the pictures.* I can just remember the form of Thom, a wisp, a whisper of a man. This woman is substantial, real, pushing a sponge quickly between the toes, up and down the arch, over the heel, around the ankle, a tickle that aches because I haven't the strength to even flinch. She moves on to the calf and shin, up to the thigh, then covers me back up on the one side and proceeds to the next, lifting the sheets, and then my gown, scrubbing one section of my body at a time, exposing as little as possible. The bathing lulls me, threatens to pull me down again into the deep, but I fight to recall the name of the other. Thom. Thom at the pictures. *Is there to be a picture show?* I ask her. *What is that? The Queen's English?* she says. *Who talks like that?* I tell her: *Thom. Or Mother. Where is he?* But she goes on about the pictures, by which I gather she means photographs. *They get every inch of you, one way or another. Ridiculous*, she says. *Naked?* I ask. *As the day is born*, she says. *They have theories.* And then she tells me, very straight, *But I won't let you in there stinking, filthy as you are.*"

"That's not the expression, is it, Juan? As the day is born?"

"I tell the woman I don't think I could do that. Pose like that. But she says, *No choice. Lucky you're not a woman, otherwise that doctor would already be in here with his sketchpad and pencils, pulling your legs akimbo.* And I must look doubtful at that, because she goes a little hard. *Don't believe me? You'd better figure out who to trust in this place. Now why would I, why would any woman, make up a thing like that?* From afar, I hear the drips and splish-splosh sounds as the woman wrings her sponge into the tin basin, then dips it into a separate basin filled with what I assume to be sudsy water. The sponge feels slickly clean as it moves across my skin. Soap perfumes the air. I see her actions clearly, though I keep my eyes closed; I can just picture her movements in my mind. I cannot make out her hands, though. Nene, I feel exceedingly greasy, feel as if this is the first bath in quite some time, and when I do open my eyes and see the dirty water wrung from her sponge—a grayish-brown opacity—I blush. Then, I think, I know this woman. I dive and dive, and surface holding her name in my palm: Pearl."

"And is Pearl the day nurse or the night nurse?"

"Oh no. Pearl is neither nurse nor mother to anyone. Such questions. Are you a good witch? Or a bad witch? You mean to tell me after all this time, nene, you still can't recognize one of us from one of them? *I never knew my father*, Pearl says. *One of those Southern gentlemen who had no scruples against making concubines of their servant girls. In any case, my mother was sleeping with her charge, a three-year-old child, and my father came to the bedroom and raped her. I've seen the manuscript of our interview, typed up, ready to go off to press. They have me saying: I am the illegitimate daughter of a twelve-year-old mulatto nursemaid . . . but I tell you I never uttered such a sentence. Where is my father in that sentence? All that violence, disappeared.*"

"She's right."

"Of course she's right. *I never thought of myself as a bastard*, she says. Though others did. Her poor mother. Her grandmother raised her. After acting for a time as an amateur, she became a professional. Her husband was a little jealous. *But for a while, we managed to get along fairly well*, she says. At shows, in the after hours, she would be approached by women who admired and desired her but she held them off for a long time. Finally, at the age of forty-one, she caved. With another Black actress. Pearl says, *She made no direct advances, but we danced together and something very terrific happened to me, a very electric thing. It made me know that I was lesbian.*"

On a particularly lucid night, Juan tells me about a woman named Yetta who visited him in his dreams to confess. The courtship, she said, was slow, at times painfully so, until the following summer when Yetta and another Jewish girl were both taking some courses at a college; Yetta witnessed a rather public humiliation. She felt sorry for the other girl because another person ridiculed her. *For being a dyke?* I asked, but Juan often didn't hear, or respond to my interjections. Yetta slept with the girl after that; she felt she was making a great sacrifice. It still seemed abnormal. The other girl took the initiative, loosening Yetta's blouse and caressing her breasts, hugging her. She masturbated Yetta, and Yetta remained completely passive. This was repeated many times. *Oh, more than anyone else in the world she loved me. This she claimed. And this I believed,* Juan said, fondly imitating a Yiddish syntax. Then Yetta found out someone else was in her world. A girlfriend the other girl was living with. The girl would have broken up her home for Yetta, but Yetta wouldn't hear that. She broke off with the girl. She didn't feel the other woman was being treated fairly.

A long, long time passed in the deep. Eventually I'm pulled to the surface by a knocking, not in sound but in words. Though I cannot see, I can picture the doorway in my mind's eye. The door stands wide open. *Knock knock*, the man says. I tell him, *I'm here."*

"Here am I."

"Here am I. The man asks, *Would you like to come with me?* But I cannot rise from the bed; I'm strapped down. *Aren't you funny?* the man says. *Why, your feet are already on the floor. Look.* A second surfacing—sudden, jarring. I realize I'm standing; staring at the wall. I lean against the edge of the brass bed frame, elbows bent, my hands gripping the side of the mattress, as if frozen, though whether in the act of hoisting myself into or out of bed, I have no idea. A face peers over the side of the door frame, smiling, a very feminine young man, very beautiful, dark and handsome. When he steps into the room, I can tell that underneath the regulation-issued, institutional clothing, is a body—ropy, effortlessly muscular."

"The muscly man from before?"

"Aren't you funny."

"Funny?"

"That's what he says to me. *Your lips move, but you forget to use your voice. Here, take my hand. My name is Victor.* I say, *I'd like to come with you."*

"Me too, I'd like to come with you both."

"Come, come, the man says. Out in the hall, I'm surprised to find the walls painted a mossy green. The doors are made of unfinished metal and evenly spaced every ten feet or so on either

side. The few that stand open expose empty rooms, the mattresses lying bare on their brass frames, with clean linens folded into bundles and wrapped in brown paper at the feet of the beds. Most of the doors are closed. Victor stops and raps his knuckles against one, then looks at me with an exaggerated wince, shaking out his fingers, before knocking again. The round doorknobs glow gold at the rims, burnished through repeated touch. Every moment comes at me with a fullness and immediacy that disallows deeper thought. I feel the questions I ought to be asking, but can't form them. The knob glows, and I wish to touch it; I reach. Victor grasps my outstretched hand and holds it in his. *These horrible doors. I wish at least they'd paint them,* he says. *Gunmetal,* I say, and again he replies: *Aren't. You. Funny.* Just like that, as if there were a period after each word."

"You are, Juan. Funny."

"An exaggerated, feminine habit of clipping through his words. He is fond of repetition, staccato: *Well, I suppose they've gone. Gone, gone, gone. So what? Come, come.*"

The moments of lucidity and connection spread thinner and thinner. At times Juan launches into long soliloquys in Spanish that I cannot understand, but anyway are not for me; he speaks the rhythmic Puerto Rican dialect, omitting consonants and extending vowels, and I am returned to my father, to cousins and uncles, and my grandmother—teasing, mock arguments, their laughter— and then as now in the room with Juan, to my anglicized ear, it's the *a'o* sound that registers more than any other, *a'o, a'o, a'o.* In certain moments, he sounds as if he is, at least, making sense. More frequent: the gibberish sounds, whimpers, and turmoil. When I was a young child, an aunt moved up from Brooklyn to live with us through the last months of her pregnancy, and continued to live with us for several months after the baby was born; everything about the baby fascinated me, most especially the idea of the deadly soft spot on the skull that must never be touched. Once, I walked in on my mother pouring boiling water into a mug and placing it before my aunt, who was without makeup, without her face on, as she liked to say, and crying soundlessly. My mother inched the tea closer to her, saying, *You gotta learn to sleep when baby sleeps, Red.*

I crawl into bed with Juan. I hold his hand. I learn to sleep when he sleeps, so that I might be there in case the real Juan returns, one last time, to speak with me. The sensation of my hand in another man's sends me down, and I drift, recalling flashes of desperate groping, straddling, an older man who took my cock into his mouth in the back of an empty bus, a man who fucked me on the floor of his closet—but I feel certain that, outside of Liam, I've never held any other grown man's hand. At least not since I was a child, with my father, and then comes the image that begins the dream memory: a carnival, only on the ocean floor. I swim down through the dark water to reach it. A Ferris wheel turns in the night, rim and spokes lined with glowing bulbs, red and yellow and blue, and there at the base stand child and father, bathed in the softly pulsing colors. The father pulls the child through the crowd; the state fair. The air smells of burnt sugar; faces press in from all sides; the jangle of ragtime blares out from the rides. The child squeezes his father's hand a little tighter, and the father automatically turns back and looks down, as if the child had tapped him on the shoulder, or as if the father were a puppet and the boy pulled his string. For some reason, the discovery of this form of silent communication between himself and his father delights him, and so he begins playing a little experiment, every now and then giving a little squeeze, as if he were startled and in search of comfort, and sure enough, each time the father turns his face, looks down at the boy with slight concern, until finally he snaps, *What is it? What's the problem? What's wrong with you?* The child has no answer. The child realizes then that the father has all along been desperately looking for something, or someone. *We are lost*, the boy realizes.

I squeeze the hand that holds mine now, Juan's hand, so briefly that it could have been a spasm, but the hand holding mine understands and squeezes back, long enough that there could be no mistake. *Knock knock. Come, come.* From the ocean floor, I look up to see great flashbulbs of lightning—a distant underwater storm moving closer. I try to surface, but I'm gone. *Gone, gone, gone.*

Juan is silent. No longer taking even water. All but . . . I open the curtains. I sort his things. Forget myself.

I find myself seated at a desk with a dull pencil. The test continues for pages and pages. Masculinity-Femininity. I found an original copy among Juan's papers. Word association. *Draw a line under the word that goes best or most naturally with the one in capitals; the word it tends most to make you think of. Work rapidly; do not think long over any one.* The questions, unreasonably drawn-out, quickly numb the mind, and as I answer I'm lulled into a kind of trance. This is, perhaps, the intent. Patterns emerge. I flip back through the pages I've completed. On a piece of scratch paper torn from the front cover of the test, I note down the repetitions, words like *jack, eighteen,* and *vain.* The words *meat, mother,* and *soldier* appear the most, at three times each. Another section is YES or NO. I carefully clip out the questions to which I've answered affirmatively and glue them to a piece of black crepe. It is, I realize, a terrifying little poem of perversion. I'm proud of my creation, and I fold away the paper, slipping it down into the pocket of a pair of Juan's canvas pants, which fit snugly. I've tried on all his clothes. Trash. Trash. Keep.

THE MASCULINITY-FEMININITY TEST

Answer each question as truthfully as you can

YES or NO.

Do you ever feel that you are about to "go to pieces"?.

Do you ever dream of robbers?

Do you like to have people tell you their troubles?.

Do you like to tell your troubles to others?.

Do people ever say that you talk too much?

Would you like to wear expensive clothes?.

Are you often frightened in the middle of the night?.

Are you often bothered by the feeling that people are reading your thoughts?.

Are you much embarrassed

Are you worried when you have an unfinished job on your hands?

Were you ever fond of playing with snakes?

Have you often been punished unjustly?

Can you stand as much pain as others can?.

Can you

sit still

Do you ever imagine stories to yourself so that you forget where you are?.

Do you prefer to be with older people?.

Do you like sex?.

Do you shrink from facing a crisis

Did you ever run away from home?.

Do you feel like jumping off when you are on a high place?.

I wake. No plastic cup of water on the night table, but there is a book. A children's book. Taped to the cover, a little note. *Know thyself.* I take up the book. If I hold it straight up above my head and angle the pages, just enough light filters in from the hall and onto the pictures, jungle creatures, a boy child, but my eyes are too tired to make out the text. I close the book and look again at the cover, where the font is larger. *Who's Afraid?* the title asks. But already my eyelids are drooping.

"Good morning."

"Is it? Morning?"

"Well, for you, nene. A kind of forever morning, isn't it? Did you miss me?"

"I dreamt . . . I dreamt . . ."

"Oh, let's not start with the waterworks already. Really, darling, you can be a morbid little thing. Where's your sense of humor?"

"It's this place . . ."

"Yes. Well. That's true. The scratch of these bedsheets alone could break a lesser man. And that lounge? Carpeted, darling, in some horrendous splotchy pattern, brown and orange and white, like someone herded a bunch of calico cats into the room and then smashed them down into the ground. Oh, now there's a smile. Now, what's this book you've brought here into bed with us? Something light, I see. Perhaps a bit young for you. Not quite Balzac, is it?"

"Yes, yes, I did miss you. Where have you been?"

"Oh, just some errands, odds and ends, burying la madre, that sort of thing."

"Gosh. I'm sorry."

"Are you? Don't be. Though there was a bit of a scandal over the dress. My mother was very careful with her clothes, you see: she had two fine Sunday dresses, and one really lovely evening dress, from when she was young and beautiful and well-to-do. The thing to know about Mother is that she fell when she married my father, and kept falling, after he immigrated to New York and was killed, at work. By work. Anyway, she lost her looks. By the end she was so thin, she could just fit back into that evening dress, which was silk, rather plain in the front, but with the back exposed. It must have been very risqué, au courant, avant-garde— all those French words, darling—back when she bought it. She never had much reason to wear it, of course, but she kept it nice all through the years."

"What color? I want to picture it."

"Do you? That's nice. Blush, I suppose, is the color. As in, first blush. Picture ruffling all along the collar, and down the hem where the back is exposed. Anyway, my sister, the youngest—a bit dopey, and terribly sentimental—wanted to bury our mother in that dress, but you see we needed to sell positively everything of value, of which there were exactly three dresses and two rings. We couldn't hope to cover all the costs, but at least that would take care of the casket. *Oh, but we can't bury Mother in a smock!* she says. My sister, you see, unlike Mother, had only ever known the little slum where our family lived, a divided house, cramped rooms, the kitchen and bath shared with other families—she watched our mother move through it all with dignity, and she thought the source of that dignity lay in the clothes themselves, the fine things, which our mother had been selling piecemeal over the years. She didn't realize that Mother acted dignified because she had been treated with dignity her whole life, until she met father. *But, darling sister,* I tell her, *the glory of this dress is the open back, the way the ruffles frame Mother* . . . Oh, nene . . . and now here I go . . . but I remember the only time I ever saw my mother wear the dress, I was very young. Just a few days before, I had been walking down the beach where I came across a stingray, the first I'd ever seen, which a fisherman had caught and kept inside a bucket. The fisherman had reached in and flipped the beast to show me the underside, those teeth—well, I had been terrified by that stingray, but an erotic kind of terror, darling, wonderful, and when I saw Mother in that dress, well, her glorious shoulder bones, the way they moved, like a stingray trapped under the surface of her skin . . ."

"I'm sorry she died."

"Oh no. Don't be. She wasn't. I'm all right. Happy tears, really. Anyway, my sister and I, we fight, back and forth. I'm trying to explain that a dress like that, on a corpse, can only signify, not dignify. That's where she's confused. But it's too much for my little sister, my calling Mami a corpse and all, and so finally I agree, we won't sell the dress, we'll sacrifice the money, anything, anything, if only she'll stop blubbering. Though it's a shame, I say, that beautiful back, wasted. And that's when my sister, she's stopped crying now, though she's still teetering on the edge, sniffling like a toddler, she says, *I don't suppose it would be proper, would it, to bury her facedown?*"

"She didn't!"

"I knew you'd like that, darling! Imagine! I carried that all the way back here, just for you. People are so precious about dying, aren't they? But not us."

"I want you back. For good."

"Perish the thought, nene. Just passing through."

A great many hands hold me down. The sudden urge to rise swells inside, and I startle awake. I must get up. I must. Or else. The hands creep, fasten me down. Already too late. *Oh God*, I think, *what's coming?* Quick little scurrying movements all around, just out of sight. The hands creep, agonizing, slow. Fingers push into my nostrils; fingers slide down my tongue and force themselves into my throat.

I wake gagging and coughing and sweating, but awake. Awake, for real this time. My heart thuds inside my chest. Where am I? The room. There's the window; there's the doorway that leads out to the hall, where the light is always on. I am in the room, but where is the room? No straps hold me down. The Palace. My breath, my heart, slows, slows. Underneath the terror, I feel weak. So tired. My throat parched. The man deathly still beside me. Juan.

What is it that the dead eat? He had asked me once. A riddle.

Better to end here: one of our last good days. Juan once again asks for the mirror. I tell him the mirror has gone missing, hold up the empty frame as evidence.

"Be my face," Juan says.

And so I part the curtain to let in a little light, take the frame and raise it, circumscribing my own visage. I lean down over Juan. He raises his eyebrows; I raise mine. He squints; I squint. "Jesus, am I ugly," he says, and I repeat the words. He grins, and so I grin. "And my, what a gummy smile I have!" he says. "And my, what dumb guile I have!" I say. Then he puckers his lips and I pucker mine, and he takes the mirror into his elderly hands—which is to say, he places his hands over mine on the frame—and pulls the reflection to meet his lips. His breath, his taste, is both sour and sugar. His lips are too dry, too thin. I recoil slightly, but stay.

"Stay," I say, to myself or to Juan, breaking the illusion.

"Me and my face," he says. "How much we have faced together." He moves his hand up to my hair, which is black and curly and oily and tangled. "Mira," he says, "we must wash and cut our manes. We're overdue for a trim."

"All right, Juan. I'm sure somewhere in the mess, you've got something that cuts. I'll do it now. What's the expression? *The time is lost . . . The lost are ever found again . . .*"

But for a moment Juan holds the frame and will not let me go.

BLINKERED ENDNOTES

Juan once told me that Carl Jung had a Latin quotation carved into the stone lintel above his front door, which translated as BIDDEN OR UNBIDDEN, GOD IS HERE. *If he'd had the resources—if he'd ever owned a home—Juan would have liked to carve a similar message above his own door, only tweaked:* BIDDEN OR FORBIDDEN, YESTERDAY IS HERE. *I told him I'd put it on his gravestone, then regretted the joke.* Do you remember visits to the optometrist, nene? How they'd hold a finger on one side of your temple, and slowly move it forward? The past is always surfacing, always lurking, just there, in your peripheral vision. *But I told him I didn't know how to look at the past. When I tried, I felt blinkered, the way racehorses, or workhorses, are forced to wear blinkers—in order to focus them, to prevent them from sensing what's coming up behind and getting spooked. Then Juan died and left me with all these documents and photos and medical texts, glimpses of sublimated history, but when I tried to pull out and look at the past with wide vision, I found it difficult to see. So these endnotes are not scholarly, but personal, glancing. As much looking as I could manage within my own constraints. (I can still hear Juan, moving his finger toward my temple, imitating the optometrist, saying,* Tell me when you can see. *And me laughing it off. But he goes on, insisting,* Now? Now can you see? *And I'm laughing and laughing, because we're lying in the dark.)*

3 *"Poetry loses some of its charm"*: Unlike the rest of the erasures, which all come from *Sex Variants: A Study of Homosexual Patterns*, the source text here is the preface to an entirely different book called *Sex Variant Women in Literature*, by Jeannette H. Foster, published in 1956. *Lesbians in Literature* might seem a clearer and more obvious choice for a title, but Foster chose the term *sex variant women* very deliberately in order to align the book with scientific inquiry and perhaps evade censure. This is why Dr. George W. Henry, a scientist, wrote the preface to a work of literary criticism. The book surveys representations of queer desire between women in literature—beginning with Sappho and the biblical story of Ruth, and ending with 1951's *The Price of Salt*. I doubt Dr. Henry ever read many of the books Foster investigates, beyond the Bible. This erasure is meant to serve as an epigraph.

Another epigraph I considered was this quote from Erving Goffman's *Stigma*:

> It is important to stress that, in America at least, no matter how small and how badly off a particular stigmatized category is, the viewpoint of its members is likely to be given public presentation of some kind. It can thus be said that Americans who are stigmatized tend to live in a literarily-defined world, however uncultured they might be. If they don't read books on the situation of persons like themselves, they at least read magazines and see movies; and where they don't do these, then they listen to local, vocal associates. An intellectually worked-up version of their point of view is thus available to most stigmatized persons. A comment is here required about those who come to serve as representatives of a stigmatized category. Starting out as someone who is a little more vocal, a little better known, or a little better connected than his fellow sufferers, a stigmatized person may find that the "movement" has absorbed his whole day, and that he has become a professional.

(I especially like the connotations of the word *professional* here, a word often used as euphemism for *whore*.)

Both Jeannette Foster's book—which tracks down every mention of queer desire she can find between women—and this passage from Goffman touch on something central to the project I inherited. Juan had pushed me to grasp two concepts: (1) the idea that stigmatized persons live in a literarily defined world; and (2) the value of getting lost, or absorbed—sometimes haunted, sometimes enriched—by what's been said and written about you and your kind, and what's been erased or suppressed.

6   *Image of naked man and book*: Arthur Tress, *The Book Dealer*. This is from a series shot in the old ruins of the Christopher Street Piers. Mythic cruising grounds, which to my generation stand as a kind of lost Atlantis, or the Garden, perhaps, from which we've been expelled. In another, nearly identical photo, the suited man stands in the same position; the book is splayed open, but the man on the desk is not. The younger man is still naked and still supporting the book, but curled into the fetal position. That photo is titled *Blue Collar Fantasy*. I wondered if Tress meant the fantasy belonged to the older man in the suit, a fantasy of ownership perhaps, or whether

the implication is that the fantasy belongs to the young man, the blue-collar man, who wishes to be made naked, opened, and read.

7, 21 "I had never meant to keep my promise" and "I came to Comala because I had been told": With these lines, and the preceding allusion to squeezing mother's hands, Juan is remembering (and the narrative is mirroring) the first page of the novel *Pedro Páramo*, which Susan Sontag says has the burnished quality of a fairy tale. "But," she adds, "the limpid opening of the book is only the first move. In fact, *Pedro Páramo* is a far more complex narrative than its beginning suggests. The novel's premise . . . mutates into a multi-voiced sojourn in hell."

25 *Blurred image of young man lying in the grass*: This photograph, taken by Thomas Painter, maybe, could be Juan, though it could be anyone. For my part, the picture reminds me of a night I spent in Prospect Park. A summer night. I slept at the foot of a tree. I'd been to a party—I must have assumed someone would pick me up and take me home with them, but my plan hadn't panned out. I wasn't living in one particular place at that moment, but bouncing around; I had keys to nowhere. In the morning, I met up with a friend from out of town, a very new friend. I had worn white denim jeans to the party and a white sleeveless shirt, which was now stretched and dirty. I was ravenous; I asked my new friend to buy me a slice of pizza. Whatever she thought was going on with me, she didn't ask, and didn't blink at the request. Today, she's a well-known writer. Back then, we were just kids.

32 *Image of nurse*: Here the nurse is testing out electronic equipment designed to monitor various patient data at a psychiatric hospital.

39 *Image of Francisco Moncion wearing shorts and standing in profile against a background of silver foil*: The photograph is by Carl Van Vechten. (Juan taught me that one recourse we have in despair is to look at the photographs of Carl Van Vechten; to remind ourselves there have been other worlds, and so there will be.) Moncion was a very famous ballet dancer, and a gay icon. He was born in the Dominican Republic but grew up in the United States. Moncion danced with Nicholas Magallanes, part of Balanchine's Ballet Society. Juan was in love with both men, from a distance—from photographs.

42 "A young hoodlum who": From *Saint Genet: Actor and Martyr* by Jean-Paul Sartre. The line comes from a paragraph where Sartre, using a metaphor that mixes the sexual with the literary, conflates Genet himself with his books, and readers with pimps: "His proce-

dure has not varied since the time when he was a young hoodlum who let himself be taken by the Pimps in order to steal their ego. He lets himself be taken by the readers: there he is on the shelf of a bookcase, someone takes him down, carries him away, opens him. 'I am going to see,' says the right-thinking man, 'what this chap is all about.' But the one who thought he was taking is suddenly taken."

46 *"Yo creo que"*: Ezra Pound. This is from near the beginning of "Canto LXXXI." I'm not sure I ever would have remembered exactly what Juan said to me that day, let alone been able to track down the reference, but in the last days, when there was much delirium and rambling, Juan had chanted to himself (or, I suppose, to me) other lines from that same canto, which did stick firmly in my mind, because of the way he recited them, the repetition, similar to the way one prays on the rosary. "What thou lovest well remains . . . the rest is dross . . . What thou lov'st well shall not be reft from thee . . . What thou lov'st well is thy true heritage . . . What thou lov'st well shall not be reft from thee . . ." And of course, from that same canto come the lines with which he'd tease me: "Pull down thy vanity . . . I say pull down!" He never spoke of Pound directly, neither his fascism nor his talents, beyond quoting from Elizabeth Bishop's "Visits to St. Elizabeths," which I misheard as "tell the time of the wretched man that lies in the house of Bedlam" and misunderstood to be a command; I thought Juan spoke to me of himself.

54 *Illustration of young boy with his sisters*: From *Manuelito of Costa Rica*, written by Pachita Crespi and illustrated by Zhenya Gay. Crespi was a painter as well as an author, and something of a known figure, I think, in queer circles. (Apparently James Schuyler would sometimes sign his letters to Ashbery and others with "drag names," among them Pachita Crespi.)

63 *Image of man guarding Minot Air Force Base*: One day, I found myself wondering about Minot, a city to which I've never been. I wondered especially about the air force base in the 1970s. I visited the Minot tourism website, where I found this image under a section about the history of the base titled "Only the Best Come North."

67 *Image of young couple with baby*: A personal image from a personal collection.

78 *Images of nudes with blurred faces*: As far as I can tell these photographs were included as an insert in the first published edition of *Sex Variants* but omitted in all further editions, whether for reasons of cost or indecency, I don't know. Of eighty participants, twenty-six are featured in photographs. Eight are identified as women,

sixteen as men—all are given a single photograph, nude and forward-facing. The final two in the series are identified as "transvestites" and photographed multiple times, both nude and wearing women's undergarments. Several of the written narratives describe identities we would now recognize as transgender or nonbinary. These testimonies exceed the study's logics of classification, offering playful, capacious, and sometimes painful accounts of gendered difference.

81 *Image of Jan Gay*: I found this image among Juan's belongings; it was a reproduction, a photocopy. Someone—Juan, I assumed—had typed her name directly on to her body.

83 *Aquatint print of a woman by Zhenya Gay*: Aquatint is a laborious process that involves acids and resistants and emphasizes tone over line. I found the print slipped between the pages of one of Juan's books, and indeed the image reminds me of a pressed flower, or a specimen pressed onto a microscope slide. I love the expression on her face and her disappearing limbs; the way she looks both ecstatic and bound.

87 *The title cards from Jan Gay's film on nudity*: The epigraph is Whitman.

95 *Image of woman with flowers*: Edna Thomas. For more about Edna Thomas, read Saidiya Hartman's transcendent chapter on the actress in her book *Wayward Lives, Beautiful Experiments*. One of the sources Hartman draws upon is Edna's testimony in the *Sex Variants* study, where she participated under the pseudonym Pearl M. It is Pearl's story that was chosen to begin the second volume of the study, *WOMEN*. How much Jan Gay influenced the arrangement of the case histories, I'm not sure we'll ever know, but I suspect she had a hand in the placement. As Juan once pointed out, by foregrounding Edna Thomas / Pearl, we begin *WOMEN* with a tale of a remarkable, proud, accomplished, queer woman of color.

98 "It was one of my finer moments": From the story "Interiors," in the book *Whatever Happened to Interracial Love?* by Kathleen Collins. I swear I remember Juan telling me about this exact story, but now realize he couldn't have. These stories, though written in the 70s, only came out several years after Juan's death. Perhaps he had somehow read them in unpublished form; perhaps this is a fabrication of my own memory.

103 *Image of woman standing above a crowd*: Also Edna Thomas, as Lady Macbeth in the 1936 Harlem production of *Macbeth*, set in Haiti, with an entirely Black cast. The play was nicknamed *Voodoo Macbeth*. Orson Welles directed; he was twenty years old. Thousands more

██████████████████████████████████
██████████████████████.

*bronco A boy new to homosexual practices, who is normal, rough, and at
times intractable ██████████████████████████████,
████ an unbroken horse.

*brought out, To be To be initiated into the practice of homosexuality. ████
██████████████████████████████ by another person,
██████████ or fate ███████ to be considered █████████████
██████████████ to be almost ██ equivalent ███████████

brown To pedicate. A Negro locution: "Well I'll be browned" exists, in which
browned is the equivalent of *damned*; █████████████████████
████████████████████████████████

browning ████████████████████████████, a *browning* is
a specific act ██████████.

Browning sisters, To be one of the ████████████████████████
████ (Hobo slang) ████ To belong to the Browning family.

*bucket The anus. ████

bug █████████████████ *bugger*. (Sea slang)

bugger ██████████████████████████████████
██████████ used in America usually without realization of, or reference to its
true meaning, even by children, ███████████████████████
████ In rural America *bugger* is used as a term of endearment applied especially to children, ██████████████████████████
███████████████████

bull-dike ████████████████████████████
███████████████████████ bull-dyke, bull-diker,
bull-dyker. ███████████████ bull-dagger. ██████████ bull-diking
████████ bull-dycking). ████████ *dike*.

**bumper ██████████████████████████████ to be an active
tribade; usually applied only to Lesbians of the masculine type.

bunghole ███████████████████████████████████████
███████████████ bungholing, ███████████ bungholer ███

bunker A pedicator. (Tramp slang)   bunker shy ███████████████
██████████████ a young boy who is afraid of being forced into pedicancy.

burglar ████████████████ (Tramp slang)

**buttercup ████████████████ A factitious and ephemeral term
of the early 1930's; ██████████████████████████
████

*call house A homosexual brothel which will telephone or send for specific
boys █████████████████████ Compare *show house* and *peg
house*. ████████████████████████

*camp To speak, act, or in any way attract or attempt to attract attention, ███

showed up for previews than were possible to seat, and the production, though not without controversy, was a critical and box office success; a smash.

105 *Image of naked man with tattoos*: A hustler whom Thomas Painter photographed. For a long time I believed the tattoo on his inner forearm to be a hot-air balloon—a bit of whimsy—but turns out, it is the insignia for a parachuting regiment.

110, 112 "Well now there's nothing" . . . "This that I mixed with truth": This pair of quotes, as alluded to in the text, is from *The Ring and the Book* by Robert Browning. (Speaking of Browning, one of my favorite aspects of the *Sex Variants* book is the final appendix, "Slang Vocabulary," a glossary of early twentieth-century homosexual terminology, mostly compiled by Thomas Painter. One entry reads: "Browning sisters, To be one of the . . . (Hobo slang) . . . To belong to the Browning family.")

117 *"Psychopathologic Reaction Patterns"*: This and the excerpts that follow are from the first medical text, published in 1955, documenting what would come to be called Puerto Rican Syndrome. Patricia Gherovici's engrossing book *The Puerto Rican Syndrome* uses Lacanian analysis to think through the origins and ramifications of this diagnosis and its relation to colonialism. Among Puerto Ricans, the "seizures" or "episodes" are known as *ataques de nervios*, or simply *ataques*, just as they are known in many other Spanish-speaking countries. That is, ataques are not particular to Puerto Rico, but only appeared to be through the myopic vision of certain US military psychologists, who couldn't understand why so many Puerto Rican soldiers were breaking down. Nowhere does this medical report—a report which details a kind of psychological resistance on the part of Puerto Rican soldiers—mention that only a couple of years earlier, in 1952, the proud Puerto Rican Infantry Regiment, the 65th, or the Borinqueneers, had faced mass arrest and court-martial after the desertion of a Korean War outpost known as "Jackson Heights" and had been pilloried by the press both at home and abroad. The soldiers had been sent into battle unprepared by the racist commander—that is, they had been sent to their certain massacre.

131 *Image of toy sellers in San Juan's municipal plaza*: Another image found among Juan's things. After much sleuthing, I was able to uncover that the image is from December 1937, taken by Edwin Rosskam. Rosskam was sent to Puerto Rico by *Life* magazine just months after one of the most infamous acts of colonialist violence against Puerto Ricans, in which the US-installed governor of Puerto Rico ordered the slaughter of ordinary people marching peacefully in

Ponce to commemorate the abolition of slavery and protest ongoing injustices. The march was organized by Puerto Rican nationalists; the unarmed civilians, including a seven-year-old girl, were shot in the back. In an interview, Rosskam says, "Well, we got out there and we did a couple of months' coverage and *Life* did not like what we produced, oh boy, did they not like it! It was a highly critical evaluation of our [that is, the US colonial] position in Puerto Rico at that time . . ." Rosskam and his wife, Louise, were both documentary photographers known for their images of the Great Depression, but Edwin is perhaps best known for curating the images for Richard Wright's photodocumentary book, *Twelve Million Black Voices*.

134 *Image of Zhenya, "Manuelito," and Pachita Crespi*: From the back of the dust jacket of *Manuelito of Costa Rica*.

145 *Image of hustler with cross*: Another of Thom's photographs. Although the image says *over* at the bottom, I cannot tell you what it says on the back. I'm not allowed.

151, 154 *Two children's book illustrations*: From Zhenya Gay's *Who's Afraid?*, 1965. The story Juan tells here follows the plot of *Who's Afraid?* The original book is set around a literal watering hole. Juan reimagines it to take place in a gay bar. All the dialogue is directly faithful to the lines the animals speak in the book.

157 *The Palace at 4 a.m.*: This title is taken from a chapter in William Maxwell's book *So Long, See You Tomorrow*. Maxwell himself took the title from a sculpture by Giacometti.

160 *"eminent maricones"*: Juan borrowed this phrase from the title of a book by Jaime Manrique (itself a reference to Lytton Strachey's *Eminent Victorians*). *Eminent Maricones* mixes autobiographical essays with literary profiles of Arenas, Lorca, and Puig. Juan was (and through Juan, I became) a massive admirer of Manrique, and of Puig, as might be obvious from the movie-telling games we would play. Manrique's profile of Puig masterfully alternates between camp and exquisite grief over the death of his "literary mother," and I am reminded of Juan when he writes: "I've come to think of him as a great teacher, not so much because of anything he did but because he made people who came in contact with him want to do their very best. The only consistent advice he gave me was, 'Make it poetic.'" I was also reminded of how much I desired Juan, and how much I fantasized about Juan as a younger man, when I read Manrique's poem, "Mi Autobiografía," which envisions a once-promiscuous poet who, in old age, is "mummified by piety" but whose words nonetheless inflame the passions of a young reader who wishes he had gone to bed with the

poet, just as the poet would have gladly given himself to his own predecessors, writers like Cavafy, Barba-Jacob, Melville, and Rimbaud.

180 *"Starve a rat today"*: A still from a televised public service announcement.

186 *Illustration of squirrel and chipmunk*: Juan got a real kick out of this picture, and the accompanying text, and even the title of the children's book *The Dear Friends*, which Zhenya published in 1959, all of which he described as dealing in the archetypal symbols and lexicon of "closet-lesbian wonder."

190 *Illustration of baby goat*: One of my favorites of Zhenya's images, and perhaps another archetype: The soft little boy prancing around in his mother's heels? From her book *Jingle Jangle*.

193 *Sculpted plate showing birth of infant*: Dr. Dickinson teamed up with the sculptor Abram Belskie to produce a series of informative sculptures: the Dickinson-Belskie *Birth Series*.

206 *Sculptures of man and woman*: *Normman* and *Norma*. The sculptures date from 1943, right around the time the *Sex Variants* book was first published. Measurements from fifteen thousand men and women between the ages of twenty-one and twenty-five were used to come up with the proportions for these sculptures, which are meant to be the idealized norms for the human form. Every person measured was white.

212 *Warhol letter*: The text of the letter: "Percussion instruments, piano, drums, and Chinese records. Books, plants, tapestries, naked statues of Franziska Boas—the woman with whom we share the studio, and another lady who writes on nudity—very strange. But don't misunderstand me, we have our own room. We share the studio, we paint and she dances. Come up any time you have nothing to do. Its really a very arty place. Real nice. (I just stepped on a bug.)" The strange other lady who writes on nudity is, of course, our Jan.

215 *Woman in skirt with covered face*: Franziska Boas. All the photographs I found of Boas dancing—alone and with other dancers—are fascinating, though this one I love most of all. It is from a solo piece she choreographed titled *Goya-esque* and based on a series of Goya's etchings known as *The Disasters of War*.

218 *Painting of three biblical women*: Philip Hermogenes Calderon. Ruth and Naomi are embracing to the left of the image; to the right, Orpah is ready to move on.

222 *"those . . . lurking in the railroad yards"*: I took this long quote from Roger A. Bruns's spirited biography of Ben Reitman, *The Damndest Radical*. Reitman's own unfinished autobiography was

titled *Following the Monkey*, about which Bruns writes: "A four-year-old street urchin, seduced by the marvels of the organ-grinder and his monkey, trails along impulsively, ignoring time and place and responsibility."

223 *Dedication to Emma Goldman*: From Ben Reitman's book *The Second Oldest Profession*.

227 *Images of injured men*: Injured men from the 1912 San Diego free speech fight. In the days leading up to the rally, Jan Gay's father, Ben Reitman, was singled out, abducted, and tortured.

228 *Image of radical women*: Juan kept old photos of anarchists—like these two women—tucked into books. Not only was the IWW, or the Wobblies, the only labor organization of the time not to discriminate against Black, Indigenous, Chinese, and Mexican workers, they recruited women and transients as well. That is, they recruited from the entirety of the labor force.

232 *Image of doorway*: Entrance to the Dill Pickle Club, a speakeasy that operated in Chicago from 1915 through the early 1930s, where, again, everyone was welcome: anarchists, homosexuals, prostitutes, professors, bohemians of all stripes. Ben Reitman, "the hobo doctor," was a frequent lecturer at and promoter of the club. Magnus Hirschfeld himself delivered a lecture.

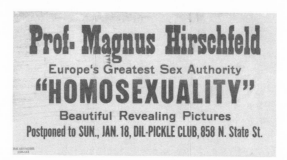

233 "Gentlemen: After a careful reading": The full text of Jan's 1939 letter to the committee renouncing Henry's manuscript can be found among Franziska Boas's papers at the Library of Congress (box 42, folder 1). A later paragraph reads:

> That is the situation in which I find myself, on the eve of Dr. Henry's sending to press his notes about homosexuals (i.e. men and women who have had consistent or considerable experience of homosexuality). Dr. Magnus Hirschfeld, throughout his writing on the subject of homosexuality, was inclined

to idealize the homosexual, to "give him the break." Dr. Henry, in the manuscript under consideration, does just the opposite. He permits his personal standards of aesthetics, morals, and worldly success to intrude upon what should be the true scientist's impersonal, objective viewpoint.

One day an article about Jan Gay appeared in *Harper's Bazaar*—the strangest thing, after thinking and writing about her for years, after searching and finding almost nothing had been written about her in the decades after her death. I contacted the author of the piece, Michael Waters. We spoke on the phone, and he was lovely. He sent me some of the research he'd found and directed me to this box of files. It was the first time since Juan's death that I'd spoken to someone about Jan who already knew the story, already knew her worth.

256   *Illustration of imprisoned man*: This image is from an edition of Oscar Wilde's *Ballad of Reading Gaol*, one of the many literary titles Zhenya illustrated.

280   What is it that the dead eat?: Because I could remember only the gist, and not any of the actual words, it took quite some time to track down the riddle. I found it in *The Journal of American Folk-Lore*, "Porto-Rican Folk-Lore. Riddles," 1916. All the riddles in the journal were collected from Puerto Rican schoolchildren, from nearly every municipal district on the island. I looked and looked until finally I found the one I was searching for, a riddle that seemed to be as much about nihilism as it was about erasure: ¿Qué es lo que el muerte come, que si el vivo lo come, se muere también? What is it that the dead eat, which if the living eat, they die as well? (This answer I had guessed immediately—back in the room, with Juan—because I'd heard a version in my own childhood, and it had terrified me. I saw an image of the dead, their mouths working, chewing and gnawing and gulping down an infinite, inky void. I saw the dead both eating and being starved, forever.)

The answer is: Nada. Nothing. Nothingness. ▬▬▬▬▬▬

A SORT OF POSTFACE

Blackouts is a work of fiction.

One day Juan told me yet another riddle, remembered from child-hood, in Spanish simple enough for me to understand, though at the time, I couldn't guess the answer:

> *I entered a room,*
> *And found a dead man,*
> *Spoke with him,*
> *And extracted his secrets.*

Then Juan died; I pulled together what I could remember from our conversations into little stories and moments, which I printed and spread across the floor and tried to piece into a semblance of order. I taped some of the photos I'd found among his belongings directly into the manuscript, along with some of my own photos as well. I learned the answer to the riddle: Libro. A book.

I left the desert and kept heading west until I made it to the coast, to Los Angeles. Every so often—with each death of the bishop, as Juan might say—I'd tinker with the book, then I'd for-get all about it for months and months and months, and then I'd remember and tinker. I got very confused, and then one day, after some years, it was finished. I showed the manuscript to a few friends. They asked, *Wait, is this a novel? Was Juan a real per-*

son? I had prepared for this. *Not all ambiguities need be resolved,* I said. *Oh, fuck off,* they said. They knew I'd spent time in a mental hospital—when I was a teenager, just finishing high school—and they suggested readers might collapse this fictional narrative with the rough facts of my own biography and deduce that Juan was based on someone I met during those months. I don't care to endorse or deny that deduction. After all, might not a reader just as quickly deduce that it's impossible a figure like Juan ever existed and that, as Voltaire says of God, I found it necessary to make him up?

Even where there are undeniably real people named in this book—most significantly Jan and Zhenya Gay—they have become fictional characters, first filtered through Juan's remembrances (who is himself a fictional character, whether or not he existed), and then my own remembering of his remembrances. The same is true of the doctors: Robert Latou Dickinson and George W. Henry. You see what I'm getting at: wherever there are facts, those facts are embellished, through both omission and exaggeration, beyond the factual. Thomas Painter was, in real life, both a participant in the *Sex Variants* study (under the pseudonym Will G) and, like Jan, an important recruiter and amateur researcher. His archive is housed at the Kinsey Institute. But the Thom in this book is a fiction. I'd love for someone more capable than I to write a true biography of the real Jan Gay; I think she deserves that: a biography based in fact. Zhenya deserves a monograph. If such books were written, there would be no mention of Juan; nothing in the historical record ties them together.

(And besides, if Juan had been real, there would have been the problem of a body—not just the appalling bedsores, but the removal of the corpse—and I can't talk about that, because you must know by now that there, I would have been an awful coward, only asking the man at the front desk to call an ambulance and standing about in the room, hands shoved down into my pockets, going up and down on my tiptoes, tracing a pattern in the dust with the heel of my sneaker, feigning nonchalance so terribly I may as well have whistled Bobby McFerrin, all while the EMTs prepared the straps and hoisted him onto the stretcher—just a board, no wheeled accordion legs like the stretchers in the movies, which would have been impractical, I suppose, going down the stairs— and I would have looked anywhere except at death, even when they carried him across the threshold, even when my knees felt they might give out from under me, I would not look, but crouch to the floor, and turn my face to Juan's library, fingering the titles of the books, and every title a trap, of course, try as I might to not register the words, until one title, *Gorilla, My Love*, would trip me up, choke me up. Toni Cade Bambara. I would open the book and read the first line: "It does no good to write autobiographical fiction because the minute the book hits the stand, here comes your mama screamin how could you and sighin death where is thy sting . . ." and I'd think to take heed of the message, and take heed, too, when she warned: "And it's no use using bits and snatches even of real events and real people, even if you do cover, guise, switch-around and change-up . . ." but what I would do instead is misplace the book, and forget the message, and only now, when it's too late, would I remember, and sure enough, here come the ghosts screaming, *How could you?* and *O grave where is thy victory?* and asking whether it's any good at all, trying to undo erasure through more erasure, or trying to see contours where the image has been blurred, or the action underneath the redaction, and why not deal in biography or history or auto-anything, why not show the past as it was or the present as it is? [Juan once said, when it comes to ghosts, you can either pretend they don't exist or you can listen.] And anyway, the one thing I can say for sure is that I never tried to tell the truth on anyone.)

ACKNOWLEDGMENTS

ILLUSTRATION CREDITS

ACKNOWLEDGMENTS

Jenna Johnson, impossible to imagine this book, or this life, without your wisdom, humor, and equanimity; you are the Dolly Parton of editors. Jin Auh, thanks for always looking out for me. The entire team at FSG: Na Kim, Hannah Goodwin, Gretchen Achilles, Lianna Culp, Lauren Roberts, Brian Gittis, Sarita Varma, Nina Frieman, Debra Helfand, Daniel del Valle, Hillary Tisman, Caitlin Cataffo, Isabella Miranda, Sheila O'Shea, Nick Stewart, Amber Williams, Jonathan Woollen, Pauline Post. Michael Waters, thank you. Julia Ringo, massive thanks. Daniel Bird, Bella Lacey, and everyone at Granta Books, and Tracy Bohan, sincere and bountiful appreciation as well. Frankie Masi, you're just the best.

Several institutions afforded essential time to write and research: the National Endowment for the Arts, the NYPL Cullman Center, the Radcliffe Institute for Advanced Study, the Picador Professorship at Universität Leipzig, and the Hermitage Artist Retreat. I am grateful to the librarians and archivists at the Kinsey Institute, the Schomburg Center for Research in Black Culture, the Labadie Collection at the University of Michigan, and the Warhol Foundation, among others. I'm also grateful for bookshops and to booksellers, and to literary communities I've worked with over the years, such as Lambda Literary, PEN, and the FAWC in Provincetown (to name just a few among many). Thank you to Arthur Tress and Sandy Skoglund for your art.

Jennifer Terry's *An American Obsession* and Henry L. Minton's *Departing from Deviance* helped me to understand the historical context of the *Sex Variants* study.

I have been meaningfully supported by the English faculty at

UCLA, as well as departmental staff; I feel extremely fortunate to work there, and fortunate to work with my students as well.

LA friends new and old: Emma Borges-Scott, Angela Flournoy, Xuan Juliana Wang, Mariam Rahmani, Josh Guzmán, and Albert Muñoz. Graham Plumb, Kristina Paiz, Sasha Rodriguez, Raas Romano, Kristy Zadrozny, Marissa Beckett; I be missing you. Jaime Shearn Coan and Arianna Martinez, thank you for the respite of queer family, and now Valencia, you're here and so loved. Ma, love and appreciation. Laura Iodice, thank you always. Davey, I never would have conceived of writing a book that takes the form of one long conversation, if not for the fact that ten years ago we began a conversation we promised never to end.

Above all, I am indebted to the Gays—Juan and Zhenya and Jan—and to the voluntary participants in the *Sex Variants* study, folks like Edna Thomas and Thomas Painter, and to the great many whose faces remain blurred and whose names remain anonymized, but who may still be known and remembered though the vernacular of their desires.

ILLUSTRATION CREDITS

3 Image created from page vi of *Sex Variant Women in Literature: A Historical and Quantitative Survey*, by Jeannette H. Foster, PhD, copyright © 1956 by Jeannette Howard Foster.

6 *The Book Dealer* © Arthur Tress.

8 Image created from page vii of *Sex Variants: A Study of Homosexual Patterns*, by George W. Henry, MD, copyright © 1941 by Paul B. Hoeber, Inc.

22 Image created from page 349 of *Sex Variants*.

25 From the collections of the Kinsey Institute, Indiana University. All rights reserved.

32 Photograph by Mario Geo / *Toronto Star* via Getty Images.

37 *Radioactive Cats* © 1980 Sandy Skoglund.

39 Portrait of Francisco Moncion (1918–1995), by Carl Van Vechten.

43 Image created from page 471 of *Sex Variants*.

49 Image created from page 182 of *Sex Variants*.

50 Image created from page 183 of *Sex Variants*.

51 Image created from page 184 of *Sex Variants*.

54 Illustration from *Manuelito of Costa Rica*, by Zhenya Gay and Pachita Crespi, copyright © 1940 by Julian Messner Inc.

60 Image created from page 919 of *Sex Variants*.

63 US Air Force Photo / Minot Air Force Base.

67 Private collection, undated.

76 Image created from page v of *Sex Variants*.

78 Image created from pages 1041, 1048, 1050, and 1056 of *Sex Variants*.

81 Image of Jan Gay. Source unknown.

83 University of Michigan Museum of Art, museum purchase, 1948/1.438.

87 Stills from the 1935 film *This Nude World*, directed by Michael Mindlin, story by Jan Gay.

90 Image created from page 694 of *Sex Variants*.

95 Edna Thomas as the Old Mexican Woman in *A Streetcar Named Desire*; photograph by Carl Van Vechten. Library of Congress, Prints & Photographs Division, Carl Van Vechten Collection.

101 Image created from page 514 of *Sex Variants*.

103 Schomburg Center for Research in Black Culture, Photographs and Prints Division, The New York Public Library. "Edna Thomas as Lady Macbeth with cast," New York Public Library Digital Collections. Accessed October 12, 2022. https://digitalcollections.nypl.org/items/3f6b9960-3bc8-0134-744c-00505686a51c.

105 From the collections of the Kinsey Institute, Indiana University. All rights reserved.

117 Excerpt from "Psychopathologic Reaction Patterns in the Antilles Command," by Mauricio Rubio, Mario Urdaneta, and John L. Doyle, found in the *United States Armed Forces Medical Journal*, published by the Armed forces Medical Publication Agency, Department of Defense, vol. 6, no. 12, December 1955.

120 Excerpt from "Psychopathologic Reaction Patterns."

124 Excerpt from "Psychopathologic Reaction Patterns."

128 Excerpt from "Psychopathologic Reaction Patterns."

131 San Juan, Puerto Rico. Photograph by Edwin Rosskam (1903–1985). Image provided courtesy of the Library of Congress.

134 Image from back jacket of *Manuelito of Costa Rica*, by Zhenya Gay and Pachita Crespi, copyright © 1940 by Julian Messner Inc.

136 Excerpt from "Psychopathologic Reaction Patterns."

145 From the collections of the Kinsey Institute, Indiana University. All rights reserved.

151 Illustration from *Who's Afraid?*, by Zhenya Gay, copyright © 1965 by Zhenya Gay, renewed 1993 by Erika L. Hinchey. Used by permission of Viking Children's Books, an imprint of Penguin Young Readers Group, a division of Penguin Random House LLC. All rights reserved.

154 Illustration from *Who's Afraid?*, by Zhenya Gay, copyright © 1965 by Zhenya Gay, renewed 1993 by Erika L. Hinchey. Used by permission of Viking Children's Books, an imprint of Penguin Young Readers Group, a division of Penguin Random House LLC. All rights reserved.

180 New York City Department of Health.

182 Image created from page 303 of *Sex Variants*.

186 Illustration from *The Dear Friends*, by Zhenya Gay, copyright © 1959 by Zhenya Gay.

190 Illustration from *Jingle Jangle*, by Zhenya Gay, copyright © 1953 by Zhenya Gay, renewed 1981 by Erika L. Hinchey. Used by permission of Viking Children's Books, an imprint of Penguin Young Readers Group, a division of Penguin Random House LLC. All rights reserved.

193 © 2023 National Partnership for Women & Families. Plate 13 reproduced with permission from Robert L. Dickinson, Abram Bel-

skie, and the Maternity Center Association, *Birth Atlas* (New York, 1940).

196 Image created from page 1116 of *Sex Variants*.

200 From *An American Textbook of Obstetrics: For Practitioners and Students*, by Richard C. Norris and Robert Latou Dickinson, copyright © 1895.

206 Warren Anatomical Museum collection, Center for the History of Medicine in the Francis A. Countway Library of Medicine, Harvard University.

212 Courtesy of J. Carter Tutwiler and the Warhol Foundation.

215 Image provided courtesy of the Library of Congress.

218 Walker Art Gallery, Liverpool, England.

223 Dedication page from *The Second Oldest Profession: A Study of the Prostitute's "Business Manager"* by Ben L. Reitman, 1931, The Vanguard Press.

227 Both photos courtesy of the University of Michigan Library (Joseph A. Labadie Collection, Special Collections Research Center).

228 Courtesy of the University of Michigan Library (Joseph A. Labadie Collection, Special Collections Research Center).

232 Courtesy of the Newberry Library, Chicago, Illinois.

249 Image provided courtesy of the Library of Congress.

256 Illustration by Zhenya Gay from *The Ballad of Reading Gaol*, by Oscar Wilde.

288 Image created from page 1159 of *Sex Variants*.

292 Courtesy of the Newberry Library, Chicago, Illinois.

Endpapers image by Na Kim, created from page vi of *Sex Variant Women in Literature: A Historical and Quantitative Survey* and from pages v, vii, 182, 303, 349, 471, 514, and 694 of *Sex Variants: A Study of Homosexual Patterns*.

1935.

touching   embracing

concerning

Comment:

punitive
inadequate   to Sal   to be the twelfth and last child o
these parents   to start off in life with
poor health and poor eyesight. To these disabilities

this monograph has been   to happen to him.
from its beginning.   embodied
                              by
a group of sex variants,   voluntary
                                              to the age of seven
when he became aware of a desire to press his face against the buttocks
of a man

I don't make the effort.

Under the skin

masculine pride.
a perverted maternal complex. I don't li
babies   they are very tiny, like bugs.
I am more   than the avera
ever, many homosexuals fail to survive the rigors of   Lesbian.
nstant intimate association with men.

I never   sleep

I love
Turkish baths, the steam and confusion, the horrible-lookin
bodies   cheap wine and harlo
                              It feels good to ha
my stomach massaged.
When people talk about homosexual geniuses I think

                              everybody und
the table   I take a teaspoonful
beer   sink   through the earth.
I can't sleep

The other night   I was in an operating room whe
a peasant woman was having her legs amputated.
Poetry
ne of its charm through the suggestion that it might be an   pleasant
on of the writer's sexual maladjustment. But as a matter of   women
beginning to seem that all imaginative writings are attempts